Adventures in the Country

Adventures in the Country

Camilla and Glenn Dyer, authors

Glenn Dyer, illustrator

God Bless,
Camilla Dyer
Glenn Dyer

COPYRIGHT

DEDICATION

We dedicate this book to our four grandchildren: Caleb, Hannah, Hayden and Joshua.

Acknowledgements

<u>Adventures in the Country</u> is a book of fiction. We honor some of our family, friends and pets by using a form of their names, but the characters and incidents are strictly products of our imagination.

Special Thanks

*To Rabun and Joan Jordan who inspired this story about living in the country. Thank you for helping us with the authenticity of information shared.
*To countless others who have answered our endless questions during the months when we were researching.
*To Kathy Green for teaching us the logistics of publishing a book.
*To all who encouraged us to write a book and prayed for us during the process.

About the Book

Ray and Ann Brown grew up in the city, but they felt there were adventures awaiting them in the country. As their journey unfolds, they learn that rural Georgia does offer adventures for the people and animals that live there. Some are planned adventures, and some are surprises.

Befriending the ragged Husky helps Ray and Ann realize that animals are a large part of life in the country. With domesticated and wild animals around, country living can be a little uncertain.

The interesting people they meet offer even more adventures. Luke, a Marine, and his dog come into their lives unexpectedly. He becomes their good friend and right-hand man on the farm and in the construction business.

Lynn, an opera singer, and Ann become acquainted as new teachers in the same small town middle school. Everyday living for Ray and Ann is full of their love for one another, caring for the animals, enjoying family and friends, mentoring young folks, and remembering their family heritage.

CONTENT

CHAPTER 1

Curious Visitors

Ray and Ann Brown's dream of living in the country was slowly becoming a reality. After much hard work and many busy weekends, the land that has belonged to Ann's family for over 100 years is now ready for their new timber-frame house.

Some of the men at the construction company where Ray works as an architect traveled out to the country to help him. They arrived with a backhoe; dump truck, and other needed equipment. Using his own house plans, Ray instructed the men in measuring and staking the foundation borders in the same area where the family's old farmhouse once stood.

The large digging equipment moved huge mounds of dirt and rocks from the hill. When the machines came to a halt, there was an enormous hole in the ground, big enough for the Browns' basement.

Throughout the day, Ray had noticed a large wolf-like dog watching him from the woods. He kept an eye on the animal as he lingered there, even when the machinery noise was so loud.

Ray was interested in learning more about this curious visitor, but he had disappeared before the other men left that afternoon.

It was late, and Ray was tired. He was thankful he did not have to drive the 50 miles back into the city that night. Eating a sandwich in the camper trailer he had set up near the woods of the old home place, Ray thought about how he and Ann had bought the camper for nights just like this.

Later, he sat outside the camper, thinking about the events of the day. Ray reflected back on the time he had first seen this place.

He and Ann had moved in with her Granny soon after they were married. Helping her ailing grandmother seemed the right thing to do, and there was plenty of room to move their modest belongings into her large Victorian house.

Granny had left the country when she was no longer able to work on the farm. She missed her life in the country and told them many adventurous stories of growing up on this property.

The newlyweds were finally able to take Granny on a Sunday afternoon trip out to the family farm. What they saw was nothing like they had imagined. It was a surprise to all three of them.

Over the years, the forest had recaptured this once prosperous farmland. Granny's farmhouse was barely visible under the vines and bushes. The long, winding driveway was impassable due to overgrown shrubbery and fallen trees.

Although the old home place had looked like a jungle to Ray and Ann, it did not deter Granny's exciting stories. She had shared about the challenges and hardships of living on the farm, but she also made it sound like a great adventure.

As Ray now looked around at the freshly excavated area, he could hardly believe the transformation that had taken place on that beloved farm Granny had talked so much about. It was now ready for him and Ann to begin building their own farmhouse.

The next day, Ray's curious visitor appeared in the clearing, watching him pack up his truck. Getting a better look, Ray could see that the color of his rugged-looking coat was a mixture of black, tan and grey. He decided it was possibly a Husky; so he called out to the animal.

The curious visitor ran quickly back into the woods, but Ray kept talking to him as if he were still there, keeping a safe distance from the edge of the forest.

Suddenly, Ray heard a loud clanking noise and turned to see an old rusty truck, puttering down the driveway. He thought for a minute that the truck was going to run into the camper trailer before it came to a screeching stop.

The vehicle smelled like burned motor oil, and steam was coming out from under the hood. Ray slowly walked over to greet his surprise visitor.

The strange driver's long, wiry, grey hair spilled out from under a greasy felt hat and interlocked with his unkempt beard. As Ray got closer, he could see that remnants of tobacco juice covered his lips and teeth.

"What are you doing here?" shouted the old-timer.

Startled, Ray answered, "I'm building a house."

"How did you get permission to build here?" he quizzed Ray.

Not wanting to share any personal information, Ray responded, "My wife's family owns this property."

"Well, I don't like it one bit!" growled the angry meddler. "I tried to buy this here farm, but that ole woman wouldn't hear of it."

Then, the agitated old man backed up his jalopy and drove away yelling, "I had plans for this place!"

Shaking his head in disbelief, Ray turned toward the trailer and saw the large dog standing in the clearing with his eyes fixed in the direction of the exiting truck.

Spontaneously, Ray yelled out, "That old man is crazy!"

After a momentary glance at Ray, the huge dog disappeared into the dense forest.

Ann's Uncle Bud lived nearby; so, Ray decided to go talk with him about both of his curious visitors.

Uncle Bud started laughing as Ray described the unusual visit he had just experienced. "That's Ward," he informed Ray. "Ann's dad and I were friends with him when we were teenagers. He was fun back then."

"Well, he's the oddest person I've ever met," declared Ray.

On his drive back to the city, Ray thought about how he would like to befriend the Husky. He could be a great watchdog at the farm, thought Ray. He determined to put out some water for the dog if he ever saw it again.

When Ray mentioned this canine visitor to Ann, she warned him of the danger of wild dogs and advised he be careful.

"He's too cautious to be a wild dog," Ray declared. "And when I described him to your Uncle Bud, he had never seen the dog before and didn't think he belonged to any of the neighbors."

Earlier that year, Ann's Uncle Bud had shown Ray an old mill located on the backside of the 300-acre farm. They were able to get it repaired; so, Ray had used it to mill the selected trees on that property.

Ray's brothers and friends had helped clear the land and build a warehouse by the old mill. There had been many weekends of work at the old home place since Ann had visited. She was anxious to see the progress they had made.

Ann accompanied Ray to the farm the following weekend. It was her first night camping out in the country. She was anticipating some quiet time out there. No sirens and train whistles. No traffic and honking car horns. No airplanes taking off and landing nearby. It was going to be great.

Friday arrived, and the Browns were happily on their way to the country. While unpacking the truck, Ray picked up a large flashlight. "This will help us move around safely in the dark," he told Ann.

Due to the bright streetlights in the city, they are able to walk around in their house without even turning on inside lights when they get up during the night.

Ray and Ann soon learned that the flashlight did not totally dispel the dense darkness outside. The canopy of total darkness made the light from the moon and stars seem to pop right out of the sky. What an interesting sight!

The sounds of the country were quite different from those they heard in the city. Here, they heard crickets chirping and the frogs croaking. Coyotes howling during the night kept Ann awake. She would have to learn to relax in this new environment.

The next morning, Uncle Bud brought his 4-wheeler over to take them on a ride through the forest. Breathing in the fresh, clean country air was a welcomed reality to them both. Ann saw the areas where the trees had been harvested, and they ended up at the old sawmill Ray had told her about.

Ray opened the warehouse door, "This is some of the lumber that will be used to build our timber-frame house!"

Ann was amazed at all the lumber stacked inside. She became emotional at the thought of building their dream house on the same land where her dad had grown up.

Back at the camper, Ann grabbed a bottle of water from the ice chest. She noticed movement in the bushes along the tree line, and thought that it could be the Husky.

Quietly motioning to Ray to look out the window, Ann pointed to the woods. They watched the impressive, large dog cautiously move out into the clearing. Ray quickly got a bowl of water and took it outside. When he saw Ray, the dog ran back into the bushes.

He thought the dog might still be nearby; so, he began talking softly as he walked slowly toward the bushes and left the bowl of water. Ann was anxiously watching from the window.

Not long after Ray returned to the camper, the curious visitor appeared from the bushes to drink the water. He then quietly returned to the woods.

That night, Ann cooked Ray's favorite meal for dinner...southern fried pork chops. Ray poured the leftover gravy over the pork chop bones and headed outside with it and a bowl of water in his hands. He placed the two bowls in the clearing, but closer to the trailer this time. Ann was still not convinced this was a wise idea.

Before leaving the bowls, Ray stood looking off into the dense forest, wondering where the dog was hiding. He whispered a prayer that he and this magnificent animal might one day form a friendship.

Although Ray could not see him, the dog was watching. He was very interested in what was in those bowls. As soon as Ray started back to the camper, the dog walked out into the clearing and checked out the food offering. He immediately devoured the food and water and stood there for a moment staring toward the camper.

"Poor thing," Ann declared, "he was starving!"

The next day, Ray placed the food and water bowls even closer to the trailer. He called to the dog and walked a few steps back toward Ann. Soon, the hungry canine emerged from the bushes and walked to the bowls. As before, he ate and drank quickly, but this time he did not run away.

He could see Ray and Ann watching him from lawn chairs placed in front of the trailer. It was as if he wanted to join them, but eventually he returned to his wooded cover.

Ann and Ray reluctantly prepared to leave the farm and travel back to the city. They wondered how their absence from the farm would affect their new budding friendship with the Husky. Before leaving, they placed several bowls of water by the steps of the camper trailer.

It had been a restful weekend in the country, and they looked forward to more weekend camping trips. Ray told Ann,

"Future camping trips to the country will have to be work-related if we are ever going to get our house built."

"There's so much that needs to be done before we can move into our new house," Ray informed. "Once the basement is completed, we can begin working on the first floor of the house."

Ray's brothers agreed to meet him at the campsite the upcoming weekend to help build the walls of the basement. When Ray arrived, his brothers were sitting in their trucks in the driveway.

"Ray, you didn't warn us about that wolf!" Dwayne yelled as they jumped out of their trucks.

Owen chimed in, "That wild animal wouldn't let us get near the trailer!"

Ray was as surprised as his brothers were. Up until now, the wolf-looking Husky had run away when he had tried to approach him. He could not believe it would be aggressively growling at his brothers.

As they arrived at the trailer, Ray could see the water bowls they had left were empty. "Maybe he will be a good watchdog after all," whispered Ray to himself.

The Curious Visitor

Chapter 2

LIFE IN THE CITY

Although Ray and Ann were looking forward to one day living in the country, the city still had its own appeal for them.

Being near the theatre and their favorite restaurants provided them many enjoyable experiences. When the weather was nice, they would walk downtown for concerts in the amphitheater. Often they would ride their bicycles to the park and watch the graceful swans on the small lake.

Living on the historical side of town was also convenient for Ray and Ann's job situations. She could walk to the school where she taught, and Ray's office was located on the same side of the city.

Ray and Ann had enjoyed living in the city with Granny. Their years with her had ended much sooner than they had hoped. They missed her sweet disposition and never-ending stories of adventures in the country.

The large Victorian house was quiet without Granny, but the Browns still got great pleasure from sitting on the back porch in the cool of the afternoons, looking at the beautiful gardens Granny had so carefully tended.

Granny's Victorian Home

Shortly after falling asleep one night, firetruck sirens awakened the Browns. It was not unusual to hear sirens in the city, but this time, all of the action was coming into their neighborhood. One of the other historical houses on their street was ablaze.

Since the owners were out of town, no one was hurt, but the damage to the house was devastating. They heard one of the fire fighters say that the fire was probably part of a gang initiation.

The Browns had heard of increasing gang activity in the city. They had even seen gang signs and tagging on buildings, road signs and passing train cars. Now, the gang activity has reached their street! This historic area of the city had always been a peaceful neighborhood. Ray and Ann admitted they were concerned.

"What is this world coming to?" Ann sighed as they tried to go back to sleep.

For many weekends, Ray was in the country building their new house. He would spend Friday nights, work all day on Saturdays and return home in time for dinner with Ann. She was uncomfortable spending nights alone, but she knew that he needed to use all the time available to get their dream house completed.

One particular night, Ray arrived home later than usual. They were eating a late dinner when the phone rang. It was a police officer. The officer told Ray that his construction company had been broken into. He needed to come right away.

On his way there, Ray called his business partner to tell him what had happened and promised to call him back once he knew more.

Ray was surprised to see two young boys in his office. Their mom had just arrived and the boys were noticeably frightened. The police officer was talking with them.

After greeting everyone, Ray took a quick visual survey of the place. The equipment room looked as if someone had swiped their arms across the shelves, knocking things to the floor and breaking items along their way. They had gone through desk drawers, scattering the contents everywhere.

"It's a big mess," Ray told his business partner. "I'm not sure if anything has been stolen. I called the insurance agent, and he advised me not to touch anything until an investigator can check out everything."

After getting a report from the boys, the police officer sent them home with their mother. He helped Ray secure the broken door before they left the construction building.

Ray returned home to share with Ann about his encounter with the two boys in his office. "One of the boys goes to your school," Ray informed Ann.

"Really, what's his name?" she questioned.

"Eric Harper," Ray responded.

"Yes! He does go to my school. In fact, his older brother, Hal, was in my class several years ago," Ann exclaimed. "They aren't trouble-makers at school. What would make them do such a thing?"

"Apparently, their mother cleans houses while the boys are in school. She has recently taken an extra job cleaning an office building one night a week, and the boys came with her tonight."

Ray continued, "According to the boys, they had gotten bored and decided to go for a walk. As they were returning to the office building, some older teenagers grabbed them from behind and dragged them to the entrance of our construction building."

"Are the boys okay?" interrupted Ann.

"Yes. I think so. The teenagers threatened to hurt them with a crowbar and tire tool if they didn't break into the building," Ray explained. "The alarm went off as soon as the door was opened. The young boys stayed under my desk until the police officer arrived."

Ray continued, "When I heard them telling the police where they went to school, I asked them if they knew you. Both of the boys and their mom remember you."

Under the circumstances, Ray and his business partner did not press charges. Eric and Hal were technically "victims" in this situation, but the police officer told Mrs. Harper that he thought the boys should serve some community hours since they were the ones who broke into the company door.

Ray requested the boys spend their community hours helping him. Mrs. Harper agreed and was glad her boys had a safer place to be while she was cleaning the office building nearby.

During their time with Ray, the boys learned some simple construction skills, and Ray encouraged them to be thinking about what they would like to do when they become adults. Some afternoons, he even helped them with their homework.

Ray eventually showed the boys the house plans he had drawn of the timber-frame house he was building on Ann's family farm. Eric and Hal had lived in the city their entire lives, and could hardly imagine what it would be like to live in the country.

Chapter 3

CHANGES, CHANGES, CHANGES

Ray could see his house plans coming to life right before his eyes. In addition to the basement, there would be two floors with many large windows and open beams. A local stonemason will use the rocks taken from the farm to build a 3-floor chimney. A large wrap-around porch was included in his plans.

Ray told his business partner about how much joy he is experiencing building his own farmhouse. "It's been a dream of mine ever since I was in architect school," he shared. "Now that some of the guys here have learned the mortise-and-tenon building technique, I've been thinking about concentrating solely on drawing up building plans for timber-frame houses...what do you think?"

His partner's response surprised Ray. "Why don't you just sell me your part of this business and open up a new architect office closer to where you will be living in the country? It's going to be a long commute for you to continue working here in the city."

Ray and Ann discussed the pros and cons of selling his present architect business. It would be difficult to start over again, but not having to work in the city would mean much less traveling, now and in the future when they actually move into their completely built farmhouse.

They eventually decided Ray would sell his part of the business in the city. He would make more-definite decisions about a new architect business later. In the meantime, he wanted to concentrate more on building their new home.

The end of the school year was approaching, and Ann's summer break would soon begin. Anticipating they would be living on the farm before the next school year ended, she resigned her teaching position in the city and signed a teaching contract at a middle school located closer to the farm.

As she was leaving the school building for the last time, the principal called to her. "We will miss you here, Ann. I wish the best for you and Ray. What are you going to do with the old Victorian house?" she questioned.

"I'm really not sure," Ann replied.

"Well, let me know if you decide to sell."

In order to oversee the building of their house, Ray was spending more nights in the camper trailer than at their historical home. Since Ann was out of school for the summer, they decided both of them would camp out at the old home place.

Their plan was to live in the camper trailer until the basement was finished. Then, they would live in the basement apartment while building the rest of the house. It was a challenging goal, but they hoped their special dream house would be move-in ready by Christmas.

Living in the country full-time will make it difficult to take care of their home in the city. They discussed possible options, and Ann shared with Ray that her principal friend was interested in buying their historical house.

The extra money would help with the expenses of completing the building of their home on the farm as well as help Ray establish a new architect business. They reluctantly contacted the interested principal and agreed to sell their Victorian house.

Ann began the daunting task of deciding what they would take with them to the camper and what they would put in storage. Even more difficult, she had to decide what they would donate to Goodwill.

Taking a few minutes to rest from her long day of packing, Ann reached for a wooden box that was sitting on the table by her bed.

Examining the contents of the box, Ann pulled out the special letter that Granny had left for her and began to read.

My Dear Ann,

If you are reading this letter, I am now in heaven with your dad and grandpa. I want to thank you and Ray for all you have done for me. I know you will continue caring for the old Victorian home we have been sharing.

During our times of visiting the old home place and talking about my life on the farm, I could tell that you and Ray were interested in and excited about those days as well. You even mentioned that you might like to live on a farm yourselves one day.

I know you have a life in the city right now, but my hope is that one day you will clean up the old home place and make it a presentable place to visit...or live.

It's with great pleasure that I tell you that the 300-acre Carroll farm now belongs to you.
I love you,
Granny Carroll

Memories of the many interesting stories Granny had shared about living on her family's farm flooded Ann's mind. Like Granny stated in this good-bye letter, Ann and Ray had talked about living in the country someday, but at the time, they thought it would be years later, after they retired.

When Granny's lawyer gave them this letter soon after she passed, the Browns thought long and hard about when they might move to the country.

The gang activity in the city increased, and they felt it was time to begin the mammoth task of tearing down the dilapidated farmhouse and clear the land where they would eventually build their own dream house.

Wiping tears from her cheeks, Ann mumbled, "I can hardly believe it's been two years since we received this wonderful gift, and we're actually now ready to move out to the country."

Closing this chapter of their lives in the city and beginning the new chapter of their lives on the farm was an emotional time for them both. Leaving their beloved Victorian house was like saying, "Good-bye" to Granny all over again.

Ray and Ann had many close relationships in the city, but these friends had promised to visit them in the country. With everything packed and stored away safely, it was time to return to the camper trailer.

Chapter 4

NAME REVEALED

Ann and Ray's first day back in the country was a busy one, moving in their clothes, computers and extra things they thought they would need for the summer. They got a picnic table off the truck and placed it in the shade of a nearby tree. It would be a good place for eating their meals outside when the weather was suitable.

In fact, they decided to eat dinner outside that afternoon. They were enjoying their quiet country surroundings. They could see Uncle Bud's horses grazing near the barn and hear birds chirping periodically. Colorful butterflies would fly by the table, parading their beauty for all to see. "How could life be any better?" whispered Ann.

Ray's thoughts soon turned to the Husky. He had not seen the curious visitor in several weeks, but he noticed a worn place in the dirt near the lawn chairs that looked like where their canine visitor might have been lying. Could it be that he had been protecting their trailer while they were away?

Before going inside for the night, Ray put food and water in the bowls and left them near the lawn chairs.

The big Husky stood in the clearing and watched the trailer until the lights went out. He slowly made his way to the lawn chairs and gobbled up the food and water left there for him. He was pleased that Ray and Ann had returned, and he appreciated the meal. He lay down by the chairs, sniffing the scent of the humans he was beginning to trust.

When Ray opened the camper door the next morning, he startled the sleeping dog. He jumped up as if to run away, but Ray's friendly voice greeting him compelled the dog to stop. It was then that Ray noticed that one of his eyes was blue with a thin white circle around the iris, and the other one was all black.

As the curious dog turned his head to follow his every movement, Ray could see that the fur around the dog's neck was almost bare. It looked like he had been in a fight to get free from the rusty "choker chain" that was hanging from his neck. "I wish you could tell me your story," Ray voiced.

Each morning, the strange visitor would be sleeping by the chairs when Ray opened the trailer door. The Browns never tried to touch the Husky, but they were very interested in knowing what was on that small metal tag attached to the rusty chain around his neck.

The dog would run off into the woods when Ray went to work in the basement. They wondered where the dog was going when he disappeared each day. They were anticipating his daily visits and looking forward to a time when they could pet him.

While eating lunch at the picnic table one day, Ray impulsively called out as if he were calling the dog home. To their surprise, the Husky soon appeared around the corner of the trailer and stopped by the bowls. He was still cautious, but did not seem afraid.

"Hey there, are you thirsty?" Ray questioned as he slowly got up to refill the water bowl and put some food in the other bowl. Keeping an eye on the couple, the dog cleaned out the food and drank the water before reclining by the chairs.

Ann and Ray stayed at the table, watching their unexpected guest resting. While the dog slept, they quietly discussed the progress and the challenges of building their dream house.

Ray was trying to tell Ann about the red heart cedar beams he was putting in the house and what made timber-frame houses different.

Ann already knew that cedar has a pleasant odor, and it is termite resistant, but Ray's information was more complicated than she could understand. Finally, he drew pictures on a napkin as he explained the mortise and tenon technique one more time.

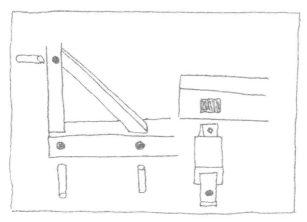

"One end of the timber is cut away to form a tenon which is inserted into a square hole, called the mortise, located in the side of another beam," began Ray. "They fit together forming a strong brace. Then, a small hole is drilled through both timbers so a dowel can be inserted into the hole, securing the two pieces together."

Ann admitted the pictures helped her better understand.

When Ray worked alone, the building process slowed down. With the longer daylight hours, he thought the basement should be finished and move-in ready by the end of summer.

Often, the great Husky lay in his spot by the chairs listening to Ann sing while she worked in the trailer. Sometimes she would talk to the dog through the screen in the trailer door. Her soothing voice was mesmerizing to him, and he enjoyed being near her.

He was thankful these people were not like the ones where he lived before. Those people chained him to a tree, and they yelled at him and hit him. Ann and Ray have kind voices and they let him roam where he wants.

Although the Browns enjoyed camping out in the trailer, the cramped space urged Ann outside most days. With a new magazine in hand, she approached the lawn chairs nearby where the dog was lying. He quickly stood up. Ann spoke to him as she sat down. He lowered his head to rest on his outstretched paws.

He was close enough to Ann for her to reach over and touch him. Dare she be so bold?

Without further hesitation, Ann touched the top of his head, and the large Husky lay very still. Talking to him softly, she began petting him, being careful not to touch the scared area around his neck. He allowed Ann to stroke his back and sides.

During his days of abuse and neglect, the wary dog had resolved that he would never let another human touch him again, but this gentle stroking of his fur coat made him feel so protected.

"What's this on your chain?" Ann asked the dog. She carefully lifted the little shamrock-shaped tag and read, C-h-a-m-p. "Champ!" she said loudly.

Immediately, the dog bound to his feet with tail wagging. "So, your name is Champ!" Ann continued. He began barking and jumping around playfully.

Hearing the barking and Ann's loud laughter, Ray came from the basement, "What's all the fuss about?"

Ann ran toward him with the dog running after her. "His name is Champ! His name is Champ!" she shouted loudly.

"What? How do you know that?" Ray quizzed.

Astonished, he sat down as Ann told him all about her being able to pet the dog. It had been a long time coming, and Ray was a little jealous that he was not the first to touch Champ.

In the days to come, the daring Husky grew to trust the Browns more and more each day.

Chapter 5

A PART OF THE FAMILY

Ann and Ray sat at the breakfast nook in the trailer drinking coffee and musing about the past weeks of camping out there at the old home place. Although the building of their house was not completed, the basement part was now ready for them to move in.

"Just think, Ann, our next breakfast will be in the basement apartment," Ray exclaimed. "We are moving in today!"

Ann had been planning this moving day for weeks. She had organized two teams: one to move in things and one to put everything in place. Several friends met them at the storage building to retrieve the necessary furniture needed to get the basement ready.

Even though the basement would be another temporary living space for the Browns, they were setting it up as an apartment. It would remain that way even after they move into the first and second floors of their new house.

Everyone left after dinner, and it was quiet again. What a blessing to have friends and family members helping them. Furniture was in place, beds were set up, and clothes were hanging in the closets. The kitchen cabinets were spacious, providing plenty of storage for the dishes, pots and pans.

As they had done so many nights before, Ray and Ann went outside to look at the stars and reflect on the events of the day. This time they brought the lawn chairs to the patio. They would miss their time in the camper, but they were looking forward to having more living space in the basement apartment.

The friendly Husky now responded to the call of his name and allowed both of them to pet him. Being in their presence was a delight for him.

Ann and Ray also enjoyed having Champ accompany them on their walks to the mailbox and an occasional walk in the woods. He no longer stayed in the forest. He wanted to be with this couple all the time.

Since Champ was now a part of the family, it was time to take him for a visit to the veterinarian. He had no idea where they were going, but riding in the truck with Ray was special.

The Browns had left the chain around Champ's neck until they could find out if the veterinarian recognized him.

Dr. Wheeler had never seen Champ before, but thought he may have traveled from a long distance away. She carefully removed the old rusty chain from around the attentive dog's neck.

"He is a very large, strong Husky, but he also has a mix of another breed. From the looks of him, he's had a hard life!" Dr. Wheeler continued. "In addition to the injured skin around his neck, you can see the many other scars on the rest of his body."

Champ remembered his years of struggling against that rusty old chain, how it broke one day, and he was free! Realizing he could leave, he quickly ran away. For weeks, he had wandered from place to place, stealing food and always watching for those who had mistreated him.

After a thorough check-up, Champ got the shots he needed to be healthy. Ray happily placed a new leather collar around his neck. There was a tag with Champ's name and Ray's phone number hanging from the collar. Proudly, the two of them jumped back into the truck for their return trip to the farm.

While Ray shared Dr. Wheeler's report with Ann, Champ was jumping up and down, barking at the squirrels in the trees. "I guess he's handling the shots pretty well," observed Ann. Laughing loudly, they called Champ over for a big hug.

To live with this couple and experience such good care was all so new for the thankful husky. It had taken a long time for him to trust the Browns.

Life as he now experienced it with Ray and Ann was what Champ had been looking for all his life. He did not know it, but he had been looking for "love".

The natural instincts for Champ to be a protector, guard, and companion became evermore apparent. He took pride in his new position as the farm guard dog, and began to take responsibility over all that belonged to Ray and Ann. He did not allow any animal or person on the farm when they were away and he was in charge.

Ray, Ann, and Champ

Chapter 6

HERO

While Ray was getting the trailer ready to move from the back yard to the warehouse near the mill, Ann decided to go pick some blackberries that were growing outside Uncle Bud's horse fence. She had planned to pick them for a week now, but it had been so hot, she did not want to be outside long.

The playful Husky would run back and forth between Ann and Ray, wanting to be with both of them. Periodically, he would find a field mouse or run a rabbit out of the yard.

He followed Ann when she headed to the fence. She pointed to a large blackberry bush growing out of the middle of an old stump and told Champ, "There are enough berries on that one bush to make a pie."

Champ ran straight toward the bush as if he understood which one Ann was pointing out. He started circling the stump and sniffing at the bush. When Ann arrived at the stump, she could hear an all-too-familiar rattling sound coming from inside.

The curious canine had discovered a large rattlesnake curled up at the base of the berry bush. His loud, ferocious barking alarmed the sleeping reptile.

Between her yells for Ray to come, Ann was pleading for the inquisitive dog to get back.

He was well aware of the potential threat this rattlesnake was to Ann and himself. He continued barking and lunging toward the blackberry bush as if challenging the snake to come out of the stump.

Angry and ready to protect itself, the snake's entire 6-feet-long body emerged from the stump. It quickly coiled up its thick body with his head pulled back, fully committed to the fight. Her brave pet bounded to Ann's side, putting himself between her and the snake.

The calculating Husky then began circling the reptile, jumping back each time, avoiding the snake's strikes by inches. He was too busy to heed Ann's demands to get away. He was waiting for the moment that the snake would extend its full length, so that he could grab it.

Like a flash of lightning, Champ lunged in and grabbed the rattlesnake behind his massive head, clamping down with every ounce of his strength. He began shaking his head from side to side, slinging the snake around until the snake's head separated from its body.

Ray arrived just in time to see that one of the snake's fangs was hanging from Champ's lip. He had kept Ann from danger, but their fearless watchdog needed help now. With glove-covered hands, Ray carefully removed the snake's head from Champ's mouth.

He quickly lifted Champ into his arms and ran to the truck. Ann sat in the back of the truck trying to calm her hero. His lips had already begun to swell and there was no time to lose.

Dr. Wheeler gave Champ anti-venom upon their arrival and iced his head in order to lessen the swelling. Ann was still shaking from watching Champ fight with the snake.

She could hardly hold back tears as she thought about how close she had been to the stump and the snake hiding there.

"Champ was so brave!" she told Ray. "He stayed between me and the snake the entire time. He can't die, Ray."

The vet told them to go home and promised she would attend to Champ and make sure he was comfortable throughout the night. Ray and Ann lavished their praises on Champ before reluctantly saying their good-byes.

Dr. Wheeler interrupted, "Before you leave, I want to introduce you to one of my house guests." They followed her to the back of the building.

"Ray, when you brought Champ in for his shots, you asked me to be looking for a cat for your farm. Well, last week a family brought in this cat and asked me to find a special family for him. Shorty is his name and he's lived on a farm all his life," continued the vet. As she opened the cage door, Dr. Wheeler added, "He's not a house cat, but he's had all his shots."

They were not prepared for what they saw when she took Shorty from the cage. It was difficult to determine if his hind legs were extremely long or his front legs were extremely short. Maybe he got his name because of his short, almost nonexistent tail.

Dr. Wheeler continued to share Shorty's story, "He's a peculiar cat. He is a loner, but a good hunter. His previous owners told me that he earns his keep by catching mice and snakes. What do you think? Would he be a good fit for you and your farm?"

Ray and Ann were too concerned about Champ to think of anything else. Dr. Wheeler was waiting for their answer; so, they briefly discussed adopting this strange cat. Shorty was certainly an unusual cat, but they were not looking for a "show cat" anyway.

Finally, Ray responded, "We've been looking for another farm animal to help keep the unwanted critters away from our house, and it seems Shorty can fit that requirement. We'll take him."

Dr. Wheeler put Shorty back in his carrier and handed it to Ray. As they headed to the truck, she gave a small bag of cat food to Ann.

The Browns thanked the vet and informed her that they would call the next morning to check on Champ.

When they arrived at the farmhouse, they placed the carrier on the patio, and opened its door. The cat shot out and ran in large circles around the yard. He climbed up trees and leaped to the ground.

Shorty examined the yard and the woods surrounding the farm place. When he slowed to a walk, he moved into a gait similar to a rabbit's hop. Ray and Ann were amazed at his agility and athletic ability.

It was unusual being the only animal on a farm. Shorty liked not having all kinds of farm animals in his way. Little did he know that his "only animal" status would soon end.

The carrier door was open that night so the cat could come and go at will. He wasted no time impressing his new owners. Ann found a dead field mouse in front of the basement door the following morning.

Shorty

"I guess this is Shorty's way of thanking us for bringing him to our farm," Ann told Ray when he came into the kitchen for breakfast.

When the Browns called Dr. Wheeler, they were pleased to find out that Champ was recovering well. The vet wanted to keep him another day or so to allow him to get his full strength back. She laughingly added, "That will also give Shorty some time to get adjusted to your farm before Champ arrives."

Ray and Ann discussed the potential catastrophe of having Shorty there when Champ returned. They decided it would take some time of adjustment, but they felt things would be okay with both pets on the farm.

At the veterinarian hospital, Champ was feeling all cooped up. He missed the freedom to roam on the farm. He wondered how Ray and Ann were managing the farm without him. He was looking forward to his return to the farm.

Ray split the old stump into multiple pieces and threw them into the woodpile. He left all the berries on the blackberry bush although Ann was no longer interested in baking a pie.

Although Ray tried to tell Champ about Shorty on their way back to the farm, Champ was shocked to see the new addition to his farm family. He was not happy to share Ray and Ann with another pet.

Trying to stay away from Champ, Shorty mostly kept to himself. Eventually, their paths crossed, and Champ took the opportunity to grab and pin him down with his heavy paws.

Ray just happened to be outside and saw what happened. He yelled loudly, "Champ! Let Shorty go!"

The huge Husky froze. He had never before heard that tone of voice coming from Ray. Flashes of the angry words and yelling curses he had endured in the past quickly passed through his mind.

Immediately, Ray began talking to Champ, explaining that Shorty was part of the family now, and he could not hurt the cat. That familiar, kind voice of Ray's broke through Champ's animal instinct, and he released Shorty. What a frightening experience for the shy cat, but the two of them became playmates in the days ahead.

Ray and Ann's patience and tender instructions helped Champ learn about respect, trust and reliability.

Chapter 7

AUTUMN IS HERE

It was a good thing Ray had built two bedrooms in the basement. They were expecting out-of-state company in a couple of weeks. Ray's brother-in-law, Will, was coming to help him construct the first floor of their farmhouse.

Will loved being outdoors and this project of reclaiming the old farm place was captivating to him. He and Ray's sister lived in Tennessee, and they were not able to visit as often as they would like. Will had planned to stay and build for two weeks. His son, Daniel, had a finance business in a nearby city and would join them the second week.

Will and Daniel were experienced builders. They had helped Will's father build timber-frame barns for years. Ray loved Will like a brother, and was so excited to get this kind of help!

They measured and cut the timbers, and the building process progressed quickly. With good weather and extra people helping, they managed to complete the first floor of the new farmhouse before Will and Daniel said their good-byes.

One more floor and roofing on the house was yet to be completed, but it was so much closer to that big "Open House" celebration they were planning for the week before Christmas.

It was time for Ann to get her new schoolroom prepared for the students who would be returning to school soon. All the teachers at the new school were helpful and welcomed her to the staff.

Ann looked up from her lesson plans when a custodian entered her schoolroom. She could hardly believe her eyes! It was Mrs. Harper, Eric and Hal's mom. "What are you doing here?" she burst with excitement.

Mrs. Harper briefly shared with Ann how the gang activity in the city has gotten so much worse. Now that both boys are in high school, she wanted them to be in a smaller school and one that has less gang activity. When she received the head custodian position at the middle school, Mrs. Harper moved her family to the country.

"They have already made friends with some neighborhood boys, and both of them are presently at football practice," Mrs. Harper shared with Ann.

"Oh, they'll like Coach Cal," Ann exclaimed. "He goes to our church, and all the youth there are always talking with him."

She asked Mrs. Harper to greet the boys for her. Ann looked forward to seeing Hal and Eric again...maybe they could even come out to the farm soon.

Ray was also excited that the Harper family now lives nearby. He missed those times with the boys, and could hardly wait to invite them out to the farm. He would like to teach them all about building a timber frame house, and they could save him time and effort by bringing up the timbers and handing him tools.

Hal and Eric talked often of how much they appreciated the time Ray had spent with them. At the time, they had no idea they too would be leaving the city.

Although they were busy with football practice, they agreed to help Ray at the farmhouse. The wages they earned gave them some spending money of their own.

Ray's friends and brothers were busy with their own jobs and had less time to help him with the house during the weekdays. Saturdays continued to be long, busy days, trying to get the timber-frame house completed.

On Fridays, Ann and Ray managed to make time to attend the football games, supporting the Harper boys and Coach Cal. It was a good break from all of the house construction.

Ann's mom, Milly, hosted a Thanksgiving dinner for the extended family. There was a feast for all to enjoy. Uncle Bud and Aunt Paula always brought the desserts.

There were pies, cakes and cobblers. Although all of the desserts were delicious, Ray's favorite was the pecan pies. He had helped Uncle Bud gather the pecans from the pecan grove that grew in his front yard.

After all the other family members had left, Milly asked Ann if she would go with her the following day to pick out a puppy.

"A puppy...what made you decide to get a puppy?" Ann questioned.

"When your brother took over the cattle farm, and Solo stayed to help him with the cows, I grew so fond of him. He was like a member of the family," Milly began.

Ann's mind drifted back to the days when she would watch Jim's Border collie "working the herd". Solo would place himself in a strategic area where he could view all of the cows with an intense gaze.

If any of the cows strayed, Solo would make a sweeping outrun to move them back into the herd. You could see him crouching and creeping toward any suspected enemy, and then his explosive burst of focused energy would propel him toward the object.

Earlier that year, he died in a vicious fight with a rabid skunk. "He was not only a great herding dog but a kind pet as well." Ann's mom added.

"It's so lonesome around here without your dad." Milly continued, "A friend of mine suggested I consider getting a Pyrenees puppy. If trained properly, they are gentle, loyal and make great companions. I think having a dog would make me feel safer too."

Ann agreed to take her mom to the kennel where Milly's friend directed she visit. They were amazed at all the variety of breeds of dogs at this kennel.

All their Pyrenees puppies were purebred, and they were so cute. Ann's mom quickly picked out a female. "I'm going to call her Snowball," Milly volunteered as the breeder filled out her official registration papers.

He proceeded to inform them how to care for Snowball. "A weekly exam of her eyes, ears, and mouth will help you spot potential health problems early. Her beautiful white coat keeps her cool, and you will want to brush her regularly. You will not have to bathe her more than once every couple months since her coat will shed dirt."

The breeder advised, "Pyrenees are intuitive and have memories like elephants. They need consistent, gentle positive reinforcement."

"Crate training at a young age will help Snowball accept confinement if she ever needs to be boarded or hospitalized, but don't keep her in the crate more than a few hours except when she's sleeping at night."

Instructions continued, "Pyrenees are great hiking partners, but you will need to 'leash train' them when they are puppies. Snowball will become a very large, strong dog."

Armed with all this information and the address of a dog trainer, they left the kennel with Snowball. Ray met them at the Pet Store so he could transport the huge dog crate in the back of his truck.

Young Snowball

Setting up Snowball's crate took all three of them, but Ray and Ann enjoyed playing with the puppy while Milly got her food ready. There was no doubt that having Snowball in the family would be a new adventure for Ann's mom and the family.

Chapter 8

CHRISTMAS CELEBRATIONS

Ray had planned an "Open House" for his new architect business to coincide with the completion of their dream house. Showing off their own house to potential customers would helped them see what a timber-frame house could look like.

Many of the men who had helped Ray meet his goal were present on the day of completion. Ann heard a loud jubilant shout from all of them when the roof and outside walls were completed!

Christmas was approaching, and there was still much to do. Ann organized "moving-in teams", and they went to work immediately. Just as she had done with the basement, Ann enjoyed decorating and making the first and second floors of their farmhouse their home. There was plenty of room for her to display Granny's quilts and antiques, creating an organized yet comfortable environment.

Ann's mom came to help her turn their house into a Christmas paradise and bring in the Yuletide. They placed red ribbon bows and white candles along with greenery throughout the house.

A huge Spruce tree filled in the two-story opening near the back door. With a mixture of Ann's new Christmas decorations and the ones they had used at Granny's house in the city, they were able to turn this fresh-smelling evergreen into a multicolored extravaganza.

Ray managed to get help with stringing lights inside and outside of their house. Traditional Christmas music was playing softly throughout the house. The entire place was so festive.

Champ and Shorty liked the blinking lights displayed along the outside banisters on the front porch. Along with Snowball, much jumping and barking was going on outside. Ann smiled at their funny antics. Although it had taken a few visits, Champ and Snowball were now friends.

All was now ready for the Open House. Ann had put an announcement in the local newspaper and posted it on Facebook. She had also convinced store managers to let her put up "Open House" posters in their establishments.

On the porch near the front door, Ray displayed his architectural drawing of their timber-frame house. Business cards had been printed and placed on a small table by the display. Hosting in the country, they had no idea how many people to expect at the "Open House", but Ray was ready to tell whoever showed up all about timber-frame houses.

Quite a few people did come to the "Open House"! Ray excitedly showed them the joints and beams up close as he gave them a tour through the house. Stopping a few minutes in the kitchen for a cookie and a cup of hot apple cider, people were able to talk with Ann about her favorite part of living in a timber-frame house.

All who came to the "Open House" were impressed with Ray's workmanship. He had put so much care in building his dream house. There was a king beam with a queen beam on both ends of the house. The white timber beams exposed inside the house allowed one to see almost the entire first floor from the second floor balcony.

The massive rock fireplace, located on the main floor, beckoned all come warm by its fire. The mantel taken from Granny's old farmhouse fit perfectly over the basement fireplace. All three floors were now warm and inviting.

The "Open House" was a success! Several couples shared that they already had land and were interested in building in the spring. Many left their contact information on the display table. Ray would follow up with these potential customers after the Christmas holidays.

Ray and Ann invited their families to a Christmas Eve party. It was the first time some of them had seen the Brown's new house completely built and decorated. It was a time for Ray to thank all who had helped him clear the land, harvest and mill the trees, and build their dream house.

He voiced a special prayer of thanksgiving as they remembered the many work-hours that had gone into the completion of this magnificent edifice. The Browns were looking forward to experiencing their own adventures in the country.

The following morning, Ray and Ann awakened to a white Christmas. About three inches of snow had fallen during the night. They celebrated Christmas Day with Champ and Shorty by giving them new animal toys.

Although their two farm animals appreciated these thoughtful gifts, they must have decided playing in the snow was more fun.

Ray and Ann joined their pets outside. Making snow angels and throwing snowballs reminded them of their childhood. Before retiring inside, the Browns made their first "family picture" sitting on the back steps of the long wrap-around porch with Champ and Shorty.

Chapter 9

LIVING IN THE COUNTRY

The Browns enjoyed living in the country. Their large house offered plenty of room to entertain, and they often had their families over for Sunday lunches.

Ray and Ann were busy with their respective jobs, but they also spent a great deal of time hosting parties and taking their nieces and nephews on adventures.

Ray and Ann's Dream House

Ray and Ann had hoped to share their dream house with children of their own, but their attempts had been unsuccessful. There had been numerous possibilities with help from specialists, but each one ended in a miscarriage.

Disappointed and heart-broken, Ray and Ann decided to stop the fertility treatments and concentrate on their lives together.

After school one day, a representative from the Foster Care Agency spoke with the teachers about the great need for foster parents.

Ann shared with Ray about the large number of children who were in need of a home. Although they were not sure it was something they could do, they decided to find out more about the program.

The Browns could be foster parents on a trial basis at first; so, they filled out all the paperwork and awaited the agency's approval. Soon someone from the agency contacted them about a temporary placement of a brother and sister.

Since it would be for only a month, Ray and Ann decided to try. A caseworker from the agency brought the children to the Brown's farm.

Ray and Ann helped get the children's belongings in their rooms and then showed them around the farm.

The 12-year old boy enjoyed playing with Champ. He listened intently as Ray shared with him about how their two pets came to be on the farm. The young preteen told Ray how he had always wanted a dog, but never had one.

His 10-year old sister was shy and did not talk much, but she liked baking cookies with Ann. She spent a great deal of time on the porch, swinging. To everyone's surprise, Shorty would visit her there. Sometimes, he even jumped on the swing beside the young girl. She would talk to him as they swung together.

Being on a farm was a new experience for the children. Although nervous at first, both of the children liked riding on Uncle Bud's horses. They also enjoyed riding in the forest on the 4-wheeler with Ray, Ann and Champ.

The children's time with the Browns seemed to pass quickly, and they would soon be going home. The siblings were happy to see their parents, but sad to leave Ray and Ann, Champ and Shorty.

It was a bittersweet experience for Ray and Ann too. Having the children in their home was a heavy responsibility, but it had been a joy to share their lives on the farm with them.

Saying good-bye was very difficult, and the house seemed even quieter now they were gone.

The Browns could not imagine how tough it would have been to let the children leave if they had stayed longer. After much consideration, they both agreed that being foster parents would be too painful for them. They regretfully removed their names from the list of future Foster Home parents.

Chapter 10

WHAT KIND OF FARM

Ray's architect office was set up in one of the first-floor rooms of their home. Its tall windows gave him a perfect view of the oak-lined driveway. Spring was on its way, and Jonquil blooms were scattered across the front yard. It was such a peaceful place for him to work.

He was busy drawing architectural plans for one of the two new timber-frame houses when Ann came into the office. "What kind of farm is this?" she quizzed Ray.

"What do you mean?" he asked.

"Well, Uncle Bud lives on a horse farm. My brother, Jim, has a cattle farm. Mr. Jordan, one of the teachers at my school, has goats on his farm. A few farmers around here raise chickens. Some of the farmers raise different types of crops. What kind of farm will we have?"

Pushing away from his desk, Ray responded, "Uncle Bud's horses are available any time we want to ride, and my grandpa always said that a horse is nothing but a hay burner." Ann smiled and agreed it was not necessary for them to have horses.

Ray continued, "We'd have to clear acres of land to raise cows or plant crops, and taking care of cows and crops would take a great deal of time that neither of us have right now."

"I know, but I think we should at least consider the possibilities."

"Well, I'm up to my ears in house plans right now," Ray snapped.

Ignoring his reluctance to tackle another project, Ann added, "Baby goats are so cute."

Ray suggested she do some research on the different kinds of goats and share with him at dinner.

Ann diligently began her quest for knowledge, and she was ready to report all she had learned at dinner that night.

"Ray, there are basically 3 categories of goats...the fiber goat, the meat goat, and the dairy goat. Some can be considered multi-purposed and a few make good pets," Ann began.

"I've heard of meat and dairy goats, but what exactly is a fiber goat," Ray quizzed.

"Just let me tell you about all of them," Ann insisted.

Ray nodded his head and Ann continued, "Goats such as the Angora and Australian Cashmere are called 'Fiber goats' because their wool is sheered and used to make clothing or rugs. Some raise goats like the Boer for their meat. Dairy goats give milk that can be drunk and made into cheese, soap and lotion."

Ray interrupted, "When I was a very young boy, I was unable to tolerate cow milk. My mom had me try goat milk, and I actually liked it."

During her time of research, Ann found there were different kinds of dairy goats. After some discussion, they agreed to visit Mr. Jordan's goat farm so they could actually see the different kinds of goats.

Knowing that the Browns were interested in the dairy goats, Mr. Jordan took them straight to the area where his dairy goats were located. He began his lesson, pointing out each type of dairy goat as he shared.

"The Toggenburg goat presently holds the world's record for the amount of milk produced in a year, but the Nubian goats are one of the most popular dairy goat breeds. Their milk is 4-5% butterfat content and excellent for making cheese, ice cream and soap."

Ann observed, "Their floppy ears are adorable, but they are quite noisy."

"Yes," Mr. Jordan agreed. "They are baaing or crying constantly."

He continued, "The La Mancha are medium-sized goats known for their lack of ears, and their milk is perfect for making cheese and soap." Ann thought they looked odd without ears sticking up on their heads.

Pointing to some goat kids playing on a big rock, Mr. Jordan shared, "The Alpines are consistent milk producers, come in almost any color and are adaptable to almost any climate."

Ray questioned Mr. Jordan about the chocolate-brown colored goats quietly lying in the shade nearby. "What kind of goats are those with black markings on their faces?"

"Those are Oberhasli, also known as Swiss Alpine. They are very friendly and some can produce up to 2 gallons of milk a day, but not all in one milking."

Getting to see a mixture of goat breeds on Mr. Jordan's farm gave Ann and Ray opportunity to see what each looks like and observe their behavior first-hand.

Mr. Jordan offered them a cup to taste the dairy goat milk. Ann was not interested, but Ray was pleased with the mild taste of the Oberhasli milk.

The goats' sweet temperament was also important since their nieces and nephews would visit the farm and want to pet the animals. Considering all they saw and learned that day, the Browns decided they liked the Oberhasli goats best.

After talking further with Mr. Jordan, they discovered there was much to do before beginning a goat farm.

They had to prepare the land, and build a special fence to keep the goats in and safe from predators. They needed a barn to store feed and hay with a dry area for the goats to stay when it was rainy or cold.

After choosing the area where they would put the goats, Ray flopped down on the swing beside Ann. "It's going to take a long time and a lot of work to get this place ready for goats."

Ann agreed, "In addition to all that work preparing, we will also need to get a dog that will corral and keep the goats safe."

"I know," began Ray. "Although Champ is a wonderful watchdog on the farm, we are going to need a trained herding dog."

Ray was feeling even more overwhelmed after reviewing all of the information they had collected. "Can we please put this big goat adventure on hold until I can get the two architect drawings completed and organize the building crews needed to complete the houses on time?"

Smiling, Ann shared, "Granny would always say, "Living on a farm has its challenges and hardships, but the blessings far outweigh the hardships."

"Well, I agree with Granny," Ray responded. "It was a huge challenge to turn her old home place into our home, but the blessings have far outweighed that challenge."

"Getting things ready for a goat farm looks like another big challenge, and we are going to need lots of help," they surmised.

Chapter 11

IT'S SPRING TIME

On their way to church, Ann let her car window down so she could feel the cool breeze blowing on her face. The sun was shining brightly, and they saw beautiful wildflowers growing along the road.

"It's spring time!" she declared. Ray glanced over at the big smile on Ann's face. He knew that spring was her favorite time of the year.

Before the service began, Pastor Jeff introduced Luke Patrick and led the congregation in a special prayer for him. Luke had just completed his last tour of duty in the Marines and was looking for a job and a place to live.

Some of the older people at the church remembered Luke's grandparents. They were members of the church when they lived in the community.

After the service, Ray and Ann introduced themselves to Luke and invited him to eat lunch with them on the farm. Luke was hesitant and did not want to inconvenience them.

"It will be no bother. I have a roast cooking in the crock pot and we have plenty to eat," Ann insisted.

Luke informed them that he had his white Labrador in the back of his jeep and would need to bring him too.

"We have a Husky on our farm, and he might enjoy some dog company," Ray responded. "It may take them awhile to get to know each other, but we could try it."

"If it's a problem, Logan can stay in the Jeep," Luke suggested.

His inquisitive Husky followed Ray to the Jeep. The two men introduced their dogs to one another while Logan was still in the back.

At first, Logan and Champ growled and barked at one another. Soon the dogs settled down, and Luke let Logan out of the jeep.

During lunch, Luke shared with Ray and Ann about his long-time relationship with Logan. They were partners in the Marines and served together on three tours of duty, one in Iraq and two in Afghanistan.

"Those were tough times, and Logan saved my life more than once," Luke shared. "When I learned that Logan was being retired, I thought it was a good time for me to leave the military too. I just could not stand the thought of having to start over with a new dog."

Seeing the interest on Ray and Ann's faces, Luke continued, "I thought at first I'd be a career military guy like my dad and his dad, but it's tough on your family having to move so often. I'm almost 30 years old and I really want to get settled in civilian life before starting a family."

"How did you end up with the Lab?" quizzed Ray.

"Well, that's a long story, but let's say some friends in high places helped me adopt Logan."

Ray and Ann enjoyed hearing all about Luke's military adventures, and they even managed to share some with him about the farm and their dream house. Luke was amazed at how much they had accomplished in such a short time. He was already sensing a kindred spirit with the Browns.

While Ann put away leftover food and cleaned the lunch dishes, Ray took Luke on a ride through the forest in their Range Rover. The two dogs ran behind them, stopping along the way to check out any rustle in the bushes.

When they arrived at the mill, Luke's eyes widened. "I think I've been here before...with my grandfather... when I was a young boy. But, that big building and trailer were not here then."

Ray was surprised, and they laughed out loud thinking about this chance encounter with Luke's past.

"We lived a long way from here most of my growing-up days," Luke volunteered. "I spent summers with my grandparents when I was younger. But, I think I had just turned 12 years old the last summer I came to visit them on the farm."

"Why did you stop coming?" Ray quizzed.
"We moved to Germany the following summer, and my grandparents sold their farm soon after that and moved to Louisiana where my Aunt Jan lives," Luke shared.

"Have you seen your grandparents' farm since you've been back in the area?" Ray inquired.

"Yes. My mom gave me the address. The GPS took me straight there. The old farm house has been remodeled

"Are your grandparents still alive?" asked Ray.

"No, my grandpa died while we were in Germany, and my grandma passed away soon after I enlisted in the Marines. I sure miss them. Being here brings back so many wonderful memories of those summers on their farm."

Luke wanted to know all about how Ray had revived the old sawmill and built the warehouse to dry out and store the timbers he had cut from trees on the farm. The time passed so quickly.

"Pastor Jeff said that you are looking for a job and a place to stay. Would you be interested in living in that trailer there and overseeing the saw mill and warehouse?"

Before Luke could answer, Ray added, "It may not be what you want to end up doing with your life, but I need some help right now. I have contracts to build two houses this spring. Building materials will need to be stored in the warehouse, and I need someone to be here to get it stored properly and manage the out-going materials."

Luke slowly responded, "I really like the quiet surroundings here in the forest."

"When I brought the trailer over here, I hooked it up to the water and electricity sources at the warehouse; so it's move-in ready," Ray encouraged.

Wiping a tear from his eyes, Luke said, "I came back here to settle down in this little community where my grandparents use to live because my summers with them were so special. I never dreamed I would get a job and a place to live this quickly."

"I'll need to confirm it with Ann, but I know she will be happy that I'll have someone to help me," informed Ray.

Ann was enjoying the sunshine from their porch swing when they returned to the farmhouse. Luke walked over to speak with Ann, "Thank you for lunch. Pastor Jeff offered me a place to stay tonight; so I need to get on over there."

"Come back anytime, and be sure you bring Logan. Champ seems to have made a new friend," Ann declared.

Luke called for Logan as Ray walked him to the Jeep. "Here's my cell number. If Ann is okay with it, I can move in tomorrow."

The following day, Ray and Ann met Luke at the trailer. They brought some containers of cooked food to tide him over until he could make a trip to the grocery store.

They also placed a couple of lawn chairs near the trailer door just as they had done when the camper trailer was at the old home place.

After the Browns left, Luke and Logan sat outside the trailer listening to the sounds of the forest. "This is a good place for us," whispered Luke.

A loud rattling noise interrupted their tranquil time. They saw an old clunker sputtering up the road by the warehouse. Luke walked over to greet the disheveled old man crawling out of the truck. He was wearing nothing but a worn-out pair of overalls and a dirty felt hat.

"Can I help you," Luke called out over Logan's loud barking.

"You better tell that dog of yours to get back before I give him something to bark about!" yelled the intruder.

Luke communicated with Logan to calm down as he demanded from the cantankerous old man, "Who are you and what do you want?"

"My name's Ward and I live down the road," he began. "I came by to find out what's going on here."

"First I need to warn you that my dog is trained to protect and kill; so when you come up unannounced and start yelling, he perceives you as a threat." Luke advised, "You best not do that again!"

Then he answered the nosy old man's questions. "My name is Luke Patrick and this is my best friend, Logan. I work for Ray Brown and I live in this trailer."

Ward pointed toward the mill, "I worked there before I was drafted into the Army; during Vietnam."

"Logan and I were in the Marines," Luke shared.

"Where did you serve?" quizzed Ward as he crawled back into his rusty truck.

"Mostly in the Middle East," Luke answered.

The old man bid Luke and Logan good-bye as he drove away.

In the days ahead, Ward came by periodically to visit with Luke. They talked with one another about their time in the military. Sometimes, Ward shared tales of his growing up in the country.

When Luke told Ray about his visits with Ward, Ray could hardly believe he was friends with such a peculiar old man.

"He is an eccentric individual, but I think the war has affected him. Did you know that his fiancé broke up with him while he was in Vietnam?"

That's heartless," Ray responded.

"Yeah. I like him, and I really enjoy his stories," Luke confessed.

Old Man Ward

Chapter 12

GETTING ACQUAINTED

"Where did spring time go?" Ann exclaimed. It's almost time for this school year to end!" She and Ray sat in the kitchen, drinking coffee and reminiscing about all they had accomplished during the past few months.

After much discussion, they had decided not to tackle a large garden this summer, but they would wait to prepare a no-till garden spot in the fall.

"The tomato plants are all in the pots and have been placed on the porch over the deck," Ann informed Ray. "They will get proper sun exposure there, and we should be eating some nice red Beef Steak tomatoes in a couple of months. I love fresh tomato sandwiches!"

"Can you believe two timber-frame houses are almost completely built?" Ray exclaimed.

He continued, "Having two different construction crews with foremen who were already trained in the mortise and tenon technique certainly sped up the building process."

Ann added, "Of course, Luke's managerial skills and strong work ethic kept things going at the old sawmill and at the warehouse. That saved you so much time!"

"You know, when I offered Luke a job and a place to live, I thought I was helping him, but he has proven to be a godsend for us!" Ray continued, "He's already agreed to help us turn this place into a goat farm!"

Ann smiled, "It's been awhile since we did all that research, and I'm ready to get started preparing this place for dairy goats to come live here."

Ray reported, "We already cleared the plants and trees that would be poisonous to the goats. Putting up a fence around this area and dividing it into paddocks is our next step. In fact, I am on my way to pick up the Harper boys right now. They will be helping me dig post holes today."

"I'm going to check out the blackberry bushes today," Ann informed Ray. "I can't help but relive the snake episode every time I walk toward the horse fence. I think Champ remembers that event too. He always runs ahead of me and sniffs around that large blackberry bush."

"Well, I hope you will pick those blackberries this summer," hinted Ray. "Luke told me just yesterday that he would like to have some blackberry pie."

"Lynn says blackberry pie is her favorite," Ann shot back.

Looking confused, Ray questioned, "Who is Lynn?"

"Do you remember me telling you that I was one of two new teachers at my school?" Ray nodded his head.

Ann continued, "Lynn is the other new teacher. She studied at Julliard and sang with the Metropolitan Opera for years. Now, she has come back to her old hometown. She is teaching music at the middle school. I've invited her over this Saturday to show her how to make blackberry pie."

"Oh, good; maybe you can save a piece of that pie for Luke," suggested Ray as he walked out the door.

Ray had been mentoring the Harper boys for several years now. Eric, the younger one, was especially interested in learning about goat farming.

"Goats need a very strong fence that they can't climb over, knock down or otherwise escape from," Ray instructed. "Today, we will be digging post holes around the entire perimeter of the goat pasture. That's just the first step toward constructing the fence."

Both of the teenagers grabbed the hole-diggers and began swinging them around as if they were sword fighting.

"Hey, stop that," Ray snapped. "You are here to learn something. Let's get to work."

It took them two days to dig all the postholes. They dug larger holes for the corners of the perimeter fence and each paddock. "It is important that the gates be hung on strong medal posts," Ray shared.

After dropping off Eric and Hal at their home, Ray went to the hardware store to buy the metal posts. At the end of each day, he was as tired as the boys were.

Ray asked Luke to come over the following day to help him and the Harper boys set the posts with cement. It was hot, and the guys stopped periodically to get a drink of cool water.

Ann served sandwiches at the picnic table in the shade of the large oak tree. Cold watermelon was the best dessert ever on such a hot day.

Ray made several more trips into town that week to purchase the gates and page wire. "We need a "come-along" to help stretch the wire tightly from post to post, he told the boys as they entered the store.

"The fence corners and gates have to be braced on the outside so the goats cannot climb up the braces," Ray shared as the boys hopped out of the truck and said their good-byes.

In the days ahead, Champ and Logan romped around the farm while Ray and Luke worked on the fence. Occasionally, the dogs would try to get away with chasing cars down the road. Usually, the men would hear their playful barking and call them back to the yard.

At dinner one night, Ray excitedly shared with Ann, "We're almost finished putting up the goat fence!"

Clapping her hands, Ann asked, "So will you begin building the barn soon?"

"Not yet." Ray explained, "Even though the fence is 6 feet tall, I've been advised to put barbed wire around the top to keep the wild cats out and around the bottom to keep wild pigs and armadillos from digging into the paddocks."

"It's taking longer than we thought," Ann complained.

"That extra protection will only be put on the outer perimeter fence, and Luke will help me," informed Ray.

It was Saturday. Ann served a late breakfast before the men began their task. They were busily attaching the barbed wire along the bottom of the fence when a brand new black Mazda came rolling down the driveway, stopping near the fence.

"Is this the Brown farm?" called a dark-headed woman from the car.

Walking toward the car, Ray answered, "Yes. I'm Ray Brown. How can I help you?"

"Hi Ray. I'm Lynn Wesley, and I'm here to visit with Ann," she explained.

By then, Ann had stepped from the patio and was motioning for her to drive forward.

Before returning to their task, Luke asked, "Who is that?"

Laughing at the look on Luke's face, Ray replied, "She's a new teacher at Ann's school."

"Sharp car," Luke observed. "I'm surprised a new teacher could afford that nice car."

"From what Ann says, she had a good job in New York," Ray informed Luke as he turned back to the fence.

"Hey, give me a tour of your house," directed Lynn as she exited the car.

Soon, they returned to the patio. With a bucket in hand, Ann led Lynn to the blackberry bush.

On their way back to the house, Lynn whispered, "Who is that nice looking man working with Ray?"

"That's Luke, Ray's right-arm man," Ann replied.

Sensing Lynn wanted to know more, Ann continued when they got inside. "Luke was in the Marines for about 10 years, and he moved here a few months ago."

"Is he married?" Lynn inquired.

"No, but he says he would like to have a family one day," Ann informed.

Lynn confided in Ann about a serious relationship she'd had with an opera singer while living in New York.

"Ended up, he thought more of his career than he did me and moved to Paris. I was devastated and very lonely even though I had lived in New York a long time. It made me miss my family even more."

As they were taking the two blackberry pies from the oven, Lynn closed her eyes and took in a deep breath, "Oh, that delicious smell! It reminds me of Grandma's kitchen. She was always cooking desserts. I loved visiting, and I have so many precious memories of those times."

"Did you live nearby your grandparents?" asked Ann.

Lynn answered, "Not at first. They lived in the country and we lived in town. My parents and I would visit often, and I would stay with them for weeks in the summers. Before I entered high school, we moved to the farm next door to them."

Lynn continued, "A few years ago, my grandparents sold their farm and moved into an assisted living facility close to town. My dad was in a fatal accident last year, and Mom sees no reason to continue living out in the country alone. I'm an only child; so when my mom told me she wanted to sell the farm, I decided to move back and help her get the house ready to sell."

"Oh, I'm so sorry about your dad. Does the farm house need a lot of work before your mom can put it up for sale?" Ann questioned.

"My parents remodeled the house before we moved there years ago; so basically now it only needs some minor repairs and painting inside and out. Our goal is to have it ready for listing before Christmas."

Ann offered, "My mom is a real estate agent if you need someone to advise you in the selling of the farm."

Then, Ann quizzed Lynn, "Okay, you first lived in town, and then on a farm and now you live in that same town...did you attend the middle school where we are teaching?"

"Yes. It is odd to be there as a teacher. I had thought I could just teach private music lessons, but Mom suggested I contact the local school district to see if they may need a music teacher. I took the only music opening they had, and this is my first year ever teaching in a public school. I've also been able to get a couple of private music students too," Lynn added.

The women enjoyed their time together and made plans to visit again soon. Ann offered to bring her some fresh tomatoes when they were ready to harvest, and she invited Lynn to come visit on the farm again.

Blackberries

Chapter 13

A GOAT FARM

Building the fence and fortifying it with the barbed wire turned out to be a huge endeavor and took a long time, but it was finally finished. Now, it is time to turn their attention to erecting the timber-frame barn.

That night, Ray pulled out the plans he had drawn for the barn. They had already decided to build it in the area where the camper trailer had once sat.

Ann looked at the plans as Ray explained, "This large room will have stalls for housing goats, and there's a place to give their shots and milk the nanny goats or isolate any sick ones. This is where we will keep the goat food, and hay will be up here in the loft of the barn. There will be a chute to get the hay down easily. Right here in the front there will be a garage bay to park the Ranger."

"Wow, this will be a big goat barn," Ann surmised. "Are you going to have to cut down more trees?"

"There were some timbers left over from building the houses; so, we didn't have to harvest and mill too many more trees," Ray informed Ann. "Luke and I plan on cutting the mortise and tenon notches this week."

The timbers were soon ready, and a building crew was hired. They finally began construction on the barn.

Ann was back at school, and the new school year was off to a good start. She was surprised when Ray met her at the car one afternoon announcing proudly, "The barn is ready! Now we can go get our dairy goats."

"What? Already?" she exclaimed.

"Come on, Ann, come see it!" Ray was excited.

He showed Ann each area of the barn, telling her all over again about every little thing. She saw that the ground inside the barn was packed and covered with woodchips. There was straw on the floors inside the stalls.

Ray then slid open the large barn door and opened the gate that led outside to the paddocks. He ran from one gate to the other, opening and shutting them. The couple envisioned their goats playing on the rocks and eating leaves from the trees.

"I think we're ready, Ann!" Ray shouted.

"Not quite," she cautioned. "We need a herding dog and a dog house for it to live in."

"Yeah, I guess I got too anxious," Ray admitted. "I think I'll build a dog house like the one we saw at the farms we visited. Remember, it had three sides open so the dog could sit under the overhang and see in three directions. We have enough wood left from building the barn to do that."

They had gotten a brochure at a goat show from a breeder who raised Oberhaslis on a goat farm in North Carolina. Ann pulled up that website to see if there were any available goats for sale. "I wonder if they might sell herding dogs too," she muttered to herself.

Mr. Jordan called early the next morning. "Ann, how's the goat farm coming along?"

"Everything here will be ready for us to go get some goats by tomorrow," Ann started, "but we need a herding dog!"

"That's why I'm calling you so early on a Saturday morning," Mr. Jordan explained. "I got a call from a goat breeder who has a farm about 50 miles away. He has a brother-sister pair of Oberhaslis for sale and offered one of his herding dogs in the bundle!"

"Wait!" exclaimed Ann, "Let me go to Ray so he can hear this too." She ran outside where Ray was busily building the doghouse in one of the paddocks.

Ann called Ray as she ran toward him. "Ray, you won't believe this!" She told him it was Mr. Jordan on the line.

Holding the phone close to their ears, Ann said, "Okay, I have you on the speaker. Please tell Ray what you just told me."

When Mr. Jordan shared the price this owner wanted for the two goats and the herding dog, Ray skeptically quizzed, "Is something wrong with them?"

Mr. Jordan shared what he knew, "Apparently, the buck is neutered. The herding dog is a mutt with some shepherd and Pyrenees mix. The owner says that this dog has been protecting the two goats he is selling. From what I can gather, she's too old for him to put out in the large pasture; so, he's willing to sell her along with the goats."

"What about the Nanny goat?" Ann questioned Mr. Jordan.

"The owner told me that she's just been bred for the first time," he answered.

Ray asked Mr. Jordan, "What do you think about this offer?"

"I think this might be a great way for you to get started. It is worth going to see them. I'll go with you if you want," he offered.

When Ann and Ray agreed, Mr. Jordan called and made an appointment to look at the goats and dog the following Saturday.

The Browns could hardly contain their excitement as they rode down the long driveway to the breeding farm. The owner of the farm met them at the main gate and led them to the Oberhaslis.

He pointed out Pete and Patsy, the brother and sister pair he was interested in selling. They were light-chocolate colored with black markings. Mr. Jordan examined the goats' mouths and hooves. He asked the breeder if these goats were purebred Oberhaslis.

"Yes. I have their breeding papers in my files," he responded. "And I also have the Pedigree papers of the buck that Patsy has just been bred with."

"We were told Pete is neutered," began Ray. "Why?"

"The one I got him from had no plans to breed Pete. He just wanted a pet for his young daughter. The goat was neutered and de-budded when he was about 3 days old. Pete gets along well with all of the other goats, and he's a great companion for Patsy."

The man then called one of the herding dogs over to them. "This is Goldie." She stood wagging her tail with her eyes glued on him as he spoke about her.

"She's such a good herding dog...she gets the job done and cares for the goats she's in charge of. I really hate to get rid of her, but she needs to be on a smaller goat farm now that she's getting older."

Ann and Ray were impressed, but they wanted to talk privately with Mr. Jordan. They decided to go into the nearest town and get some lunch before making their final decision.

Mr. Jordan told them that he was pleased with the goats' healthy condition and suggested they ask to see the breeding papers when they returned to the farm after lunch.

Everything seemed to be in order so Ray and Ann paid the owner for Pete, Patsy and Goldie. They were now the proud owners of two dairy goats and a herding dog!

On the way home, Ray and Ann realized they had not prepared Champ for the three additions to their farm family.

"Do you think we should put the goats and Goldie inside the goat barn this first night?" Ray asked.

Ann guessed, "Maybe. I think Champ might not be as upset if he can't physically see them all night long."

Champ met them at the road and ran along the driveway barking loudly at the animals standing in the back of the truck. He was jumping up, trying to reach the goats. Goldie was also barking as she placed herself between the goats and the gate of the truck.

Ray managed to move Champ away from the truck while Mr. Jordan unloaded the goats, and Ann led Goldie into the front entrance of the barn.

Ray was anxious to get each goat in its own stall when Mr. Jordan reminded him that although they were different genders and from the same family, Pete had been neutered. It was okay for them to be together in the large open area of the barn.

There was hay in the manger and fresh water in buckets hanging near the stalls. Goldie's food was stored in a closed-lid metal container. Water for her was located near the back door.

The animals wandered around, checking out the barn, but soon settled down on the soft hay. Ray suggested he might spend the night in the barn with them since it was their first night on the farm.

Mr. Jordan assured him that the goats would be okay alone in the barn, but he encouraged Ray to move them outside to the paddock the next day since the weather was nice.

It was late, and Ray could not go to sleep. Champ was barking nonstop. Ray could also hear an unfamiliar bark from inside the barn, and he was concerned about the goats.

Slipping quietly out of bed, Ray went outside to check on everything at the barn. He saw Champ crouched and growling near the barn door.

"What is wrong with you," he quizzed the rambunctious watchdog.

As Ray opened the barn door, Goldie bounded by him, chasing a startled raccoon into the forest.

Ray checked everything in the barn, and the goats were fine. When the dogs finally settled down, he returned to the house.

It seemed Ray had just fallen asleep when Ann abruptly awakened him. She was shaking him fiercely and screaming, "This is a goat farm, Ray! It is a goat farm! The Brown Family Farm is now a goat farm!"

Goldie, Pete and Patsy

Chapter 14

CARING FOR THE GOATS

The three new inhabitants at the farm survived their first night and were ready to check out the paddock.

"An ounce of prevention is worth a pound of cure" is very true when it comes to goats. Someone advised the Browns that it is a lot easier to keep them well than to heal them when they become ill.

It was important that the goats stay on dry land to combat parasites and hoof rot; so, Ray examined the condition of the paddock and the barn every morning. Throwing out wet hay and adding dry hay to the stalls and manger was an ongoing chore.

Dr. Wheeler told the Browns they could take care of parasites by giving their goats a de-wormer drink every year. Since goats' hooves grow like human nails, she advised them to check and trim their hooves periodically.

Ray and Ann learned that goats also need attention to their nutrition in order to thrive. They are browsers and eat grass, shrubs, tree leaves and bark. Goats are excellent at clearing rough, overgrown land, and that is why Ray left all the trees and underbrush in the pasture.

There are tales of how goats will eat everything. It is true in part because they are curious. They may try to eat cardboard, tin cans, and even clothing, but goats need to eat plant material to stay healthy.

Ray and Ann watched Patsy and Pete roaming around the paddock. Patsy was beginning to look pregnant, and they were anticipating having some little goat kids in a few months.

Ray told Ann, "They shouldn't eat just fresh grass. Hay is the main source of nutrients for them apart from their range."

He continued, "When I bought all that hay that is stored in the barn loft, the salesman told me that alfalfa hay has more protein, vitamins and minerals. It also has more calcium which is really good for Patsy and any kids she will have."

Ann followed Ray to the barn to feed the goats. "What do you have in these sealed plastic containers?"

"That's where I keep the grains formulated for the goats. The sealed lid keeps pest out of the grain."

He divided the goat food, "They need a balanced ration each day, but we have to be careful not to overfeed them grain. It can cause bloating, illness or even death."

He continued, "We will give Patsy a standard dairy grain ration while she is pregnant and nursing."

"Wow, you've learned a lot about caring for these goats," Ann chuckled.

"There's a lot to learn." Ray advised, "We're both going to have to learn more about birthing baby goats before Patsy has her kids!"

After putting a calculated amount of grain into buckets, he called the goats to come eat. Without hesitation, they both came running.

Ann was not quick enough to get out of their way. Down she fell and the bucket in her hand flew up into the air, emptying its entire contents. Startled, Ann got up slowly, dusting off her jeans.

Ray ran over to her, "Are you okay?"

"Yes. I think so," Ann responded.

Pete and Patsy ate their grain and each took a bite or two of hay from the manger before returning to the rocks in the paddock.

"You told me earlier that all dairy goats must have salt and fresh clean water," reminded Ann. "I see the water buckets hanging near the stalls, but how are you giving them salt?"

Pointing toward the dog pen, Ray answered. "See that white square block at the base of the tree...that's a salt block. Pete and Patsy can lick it anytime they desire."

Ray also hung an old tire from one of the trees located in their paddock. It was hanging at a height they could drink without spilling it. The goats would run over to the tire to greet him when he came in with fresh water.

Goats are herd animals and need space to exercise. Sometimes, Ray would open the gate to an additional paddock, giving them more room in which to run and play.

Ray told Ann, "You know that goats are never fully domesticated, but Pete has been a pet."

Pete was very calm around people and even let children pet him and ride on his back. Both of the goats seemed to enjoy visits from Uncle Bud's grandsons. Wayne and Ty brought snacks of apples, raisins, slice bread and corn chips for the goats.

The Browns sadly learned that too many snacks will make the goats sick, and had to monitor their future snack intake.

Although caring for the animals took much time, Ann wanted a vegetable garden. She had read an article about "no-tilling" gardens in one of her magazines and convinced Ray they needed to try it.

They chose a small plot of land that was located between the garage and the horse fence. It was level and got lots of sun. There would need to be a stockpile of items to help with the preparation of this no-till garden.

First, a thick layer of newspapers covered the entire garden plot to stop the grass in that area from growing. They covered the newspapers with leaves. Next, they would need compost for fertilizer.

Animal manure puts nutrients and organic matter into the soil. Uncle Bud had a compost of horse manure, and Ray had been adding the goat manure too. Between the two, there was enough fertilizer to cover and hold down the newspapers while they were decomposing.

Champ was right in the middle of things as the Browns prepared the garden plot. He would leave them periodically to check on Goldie and the goats.

Finally, the couple needed a load of sawdust and wood chips from the mill. It took a great deal of time to collect the necessary items and spread the layers, but now all they had to do was wait for everything to "break down" over winter. It was their hope that in the spring this plot of land would be ready to mulch and plant their first garden.

Having just two goats to care for, Goldie was able to lie in the doghouse and see Pete and Patsy no matter where they roamed in the paddock. Some days, she would lie along the fence line where Champ often joined her on the outside of the fence.

The goats stayed outside in the paddock night and day. It seemed Goldie never slept. She was either running around checking the goat paddock or lying in an area where she could see everything.

Before going to bed each night, Ray looked out the big window to check on the goats. He could see Champ running along the outside perimeter of the goat pasture, looking for potential enemies.

Pete and Patsy were usually lying under the dog overhang close by Goldie's chosen spot. Between the dogs and the Browns, the goats were being well cared for.

Chapter 15

BUDDING FRIENDSHIPS

Ray and Ann had been so busy taking care of the goats and preparing the garden that they had not been able to go to any of the football games that fall. Their high school team would be hosting the regional championship game the upcoming Friday night.

The Browns wanted to go see Hal Harper, now an eleventh grader, play. They invited Luke to go to the game with them, and Ann purchased three tickets at the school office.

Ray hurriedly fed the dogs and the goats, completing the chores for the night before leaving for the game. They arrived at the stadium early so they could find good seats. They were able to find seats on the 10th row near the 50-yard line.

Both of the school bands were taking turns showing off their musical talent and school spirit. The stands were filling up quickly, and there was excitement in the air.

Soon the announcer came on the loud speaker welcoming everyone. He introduced the ROTC team that would be leading the pledge. Luke leaned over to tell Ann, "I was in ROTC in high school and college."

After the pledge, the announcer came back on the loud speaker saying, "Please remain standing. One of our alumni, Ms. Lynn Wesley, will be singing the "National Anthem".

"Oh, I forgot to tell you that Lynn will be sitting with us," Ann informed the guys as she moved her blanket and purse to make room for Lynn.

A quick text from Ann told Lynn where they were sitting, and she joined them in the stands. Ann was able to introduce Lynn and Luke before the game began.

The men talked about each play made during the football game, and the women shared with one another about their plans for their upcoming Thanksgiving break.

Ann was the drum major her senior year in high school and was interested in the half-time show; so the guys went to get some hot chocolate for the ladies before the second half of the game began.

"Luke seems like a nice guy," Lynn volunteered.

"He is very thoughtful and caring," Ann agreed.

Lynn quizzed, "Do you know if he's dating anyone?"

"I don't know, but I don't think so," Ann answered.

Walking back to the stands, Luke said, "Lynn doesn't have on a ring, so I assume she is not married. Do you know if she is seeing anyone?"

"I have no idea," Ray responded.

The second half of the game was so exciting there was not much conversation. Their team won the regional championship, and the stands erupted with loud horns and shakers.

The team's families and friends ran out onto the field screaming with jubilation! After congratulating Hal and Coach Cal, the four of them decided to go to a nearby cafe.

Once seated, the conversation began with their days in high school, and it soon ended up with them sharing about their days in college.

Ray and Ann actually met while Ray was studying at an architect school located not far from Ann's college. Lynn and Luke listened intently as the Browns shared about their dating days and eventual engagement and wedding.

Lynn shared that she had gone to Julliard on a music scholarship. She was surprised to get a job singing at the Metropolitan Opera. Although she loved her job and all the things a big city like New York offered, she is glad to be back in her hometown.

Luke told them that he attended a DOD high school in Wiesbaden, Germany. His family moved back to the USA in time for him to go to college. After his second year of university studies, he decide to go into the military.

"I just wanted to help with the war in the Middle East," Luke explained. "Although my dad is in the Air Force, I decided to enlist in the Marines like my dad's dad.

"Where are your parents now?" asked Ray.

"Actually, they are in the process of moving to Colorado. My dad will be teaching at the Air Force Academy."

Luke added, "Since there are no plans for building a house during the holidays, I would like to spend the holidays with my family."

Ray responded, "It's a good time of the year for you to leave town as far as our business is concerned."

"Will you be flying to Colorado?" Lynn asked Luke.

"No. I'll be driving. My dog, Logan, will be with me. I plan on spending Thanksgiving with my Aunt Jan's family in Louisiana." Luke added, "My sister and her family will be at my parents' house for Christmas! It's been a long time since I've seen Marie and her family."

Ann kiddingly responded, "We'll be proud parents of some goat kids sometime in January or February, and we'll need you to help us; so I trust you will be back before that!"

All four of them laughed as Luke promised Ann he would be back by New Years.

Chapter 16

HERE IS SAMPSON

Ann's mom brought Snowball to visit the farm animals. After a few sniffs and a short time of barking at Goldie and the goats, Snowball turned her attention toward Champ.

Ray observed, "Champ and Snowball play like siblings. I wish she didn't always have to be on a leash."

"Pyrenees need boundaries to keep them from roaming off, and I'm not ready to take a chance she might follow Champ into the road," Milly admitted.

Ann added, "Leash training hasn't been easy, but Snowball has been a great pet for you."

Milly agreed, "She's such a loyal, friendly dog, and the invisible fence around my yard keeps her from wandering off."

Ray shared that they will need to get another dog to help Goldie when the baby goats are born. He thought a Pyrenees might be a good goat dog.

Ann's mom suggested they check out the Rescue Shelters in the area. "I've heard you can adopt even pure-bred dogs."

Taking her mom's advice, Ann pulled up "Great Pyrenees Rescue" sites on her computer. There were several Great Pyrenees available in one of the rescue shelters, and she called to talk with the director about them.

"We have one purebred Pyrenees puppy," he began. "Sampson has already been crate-trained and leash-trained. His registration papers look like he's from a line of champions."

It sounded too good to be true, but the Browns went to check out this amazing possibility. They immediately noticed Sampson's friendly nature and strong, proud stature. They spent some time petting him and talking with him. He looked to be as healthy as any puppy could be.

"How do you think he'd do protecting goats on a farm?" quizzed Ray.

"Well, Great Pyrenees were originally bred for guarding livestock," the director responded. "Sampson gets along well with the other dogs here, and he hasn't tried to get out of the fence."

Young Sampson

After seeing his pedigree, Ray and Ann decided to take Sampson home with them that day. They stopped at the store for dog food and a feeding bowl just for Sampson.

On their way home, they tried to inform Sampson about the farm and their animal family.

"You will love living on our farm," Ray began. "You will be learning from Goldie how to take care of the goats. She's an older dog and will need your help when the baby goats are born."

"Champ is also an older dog on our farm, and he oversees the entire Brown farm," Ann chimed in.

Concerned, she asked, "Ray, how do you think Champ will respond to having yet another dog on the farm?"

"He loves to play with Snowball; so I think he'll be okay," Ray responded.

Champ was running along the fence when they arrived on the farm. "Snowball has come to play," he thought as he saw Sampson emerging from the truck. He went running toward them, anticipating pats on the head from Ray and Ann and some time with Snowball.

Today, he was surprised. It was not Snowball, and the Brown's attention was on another dog.

Ray called out to him, "Champ, let me introduce you to Sampson, the newest member of our farm family."

Champ immediately stiffened, and the fur on his body stood up. He showed his sharp teeth as he lowered his head and started a deep defensive growl.

He barely heard Ray saying, "Champ, Sampson will be helping Goldie with the goats, but I want you two to become friends."

Ray decided to stay on the porch with Champ while Ann led Sampson around the house, pointing out different things in the yard.

As they neared the garage, a streak of fur dashed by. "That's Shorty, the farm cat," Ann informed Sampson. "You probably won't see much of him. He's a loner." They ended up at the goat paddocks.

Champ seemed indifferent toward Sampson, but he joined Ray and Ann at the gate. Sampson pulled on the leash as they walked him toward the paddock where the goats were resting.

Ray informed the young dog, "Sampson, this is Goldie. She is the one we were telling you about. These are the goats, Pete and Patsy."

Goldie placed herself closer to the goats when Sampson started barking. "I think Sampson is just being friendly," Ann suggested to Goldie.

"Sit, Sampson!" she commanded. To their surprise, Sampson sat on his hind legs as directed. "Well, I guess he really has been trained," she exclaimed.

They led him around the pasture, showing him the four paddocks as Ray explained his expectations for this rambunctious young Pyrenees. The squirrels running up and down the trees were a distraction for Sampson, and he could not help but try to run after them. Ann was able to hold him back with the leash.

Ray shared, "At first, you'll be in this paddock. Once you get acquainted, then we'll let you in the paddock with Goldie and the goats."

"You know, I actually think he understands what we are saying," Ann exclaimed.

Once inside the paddock that was located near the road, they walked Sampson around before unleashing him. He ran around getting a better look at his new environment. He would stop periodically to bark at the cars passing by as if to say, "Look. This is my new home."

Sampson lay near the fence chewing on his rawhide bone and watching the goats climbing the rocks and drinking water from the swinging tire. Eventually, Goldie came to the adjoining fence as if to greet Sampson.

After some time, Ray put a leash around Sampson's neck and took him into the other paddock while he was giving Pete and Patsy fresh water and filling the manger with hay. If he barked at the goats or tried to run them, Ray would correct the undesirable behavior.

Finally, came the day when Ray decided to put Sampson in the paddock with Goldie and the goats. He informed the seasoned herding dog, "Now, Goldie, I want you to teach Sampson all you know about taking care of goats."

Ray walked Sampson around that paddock before taking off his leash. Goldie wasted no time letting Sampson know that she was the dog in charge!

Although Sampson had a playful attitude, Ray was pleased that he did not chase the goats nor nip at their hooves.

When Goldie barked, Sampson followed her around the paddock, checking for any potential danger.

One day, Ray told Ann, "Sampson is settling down and following Goldie's lead. I think he's going to be ready to help with Patsy's kids."

Goldie and Sampson would take turns sleeping in the daytime, and at night, they were both on duty. When coyotes barked during the night, the dogs returned their barks. Sampson had to get use to many different animal sounds around the farm.

One night, he had decided to rest a bit in the doghouse when Goldie's loud barking startled him. Running toward the barking sound, Sampson saw a huge deer buck walking down the driveway. "Now, that's the biggest animal I've ever seen!" thought Sampson.

The farm animals were aware of the colder weather and most nights, Pete and Patsy slept in the 3-sided doghouses Ray had built in each paddock.

"It's not long until Christmas," Ray told the goats one morning while giving them fresh hay."

Ray called to Sampson, "I can't wait for you to meet Luke and Logan. Luke works for me and Logan is Champ's friend. I think you will like both of them. They went on a long trip, but should be back in a couple of weeks.

Chapter 17

CHECKING OUT THE FARM

Lynn's mom, Cindy, had a goal to put her farm up for sale by Christmas. The house was now ready. They agreed to list it with Carroll Real Estate when Ann reminded them that her mom owned the company.

Cindy showed Milly pictures of her renovated farmhouse as they discussed the value of the farm property and a possible listing price.

Milly recognized the house and informed her, "I'm familiar with your farm. My son, Jim, bought the cattle farm next door."

"That was my parents' farm!" Cindy exclaimed. "Jim and Susie have been wonderful neighbors, especially after my husband died. I don't think I could have stayed on the farm this long if they weren't there helping me."

She continued, "Dave and I moved out to the country so we could help my dad with the cows. When my parents were no longer able to work on the farm, they moved into a retirement area here in town. I've recently moved in with Lynn so I can be closer to them."

A "For Sale" sign went up immediately in the front yard of Cindy's farmhouse. Naturally, Milly was concerned about who would be her son's new neighbors, and she began actively searching for just the "right family" to buy the farm.

Christmas break was busy for Ann and Ray, but they were looking forward to a weekend visit with their niece, Beth. Her parents were going out of town for a wedding, but she wanted to stay at the farm with Ray and Ann.

"She'll love the animals, and it'll be fun for us to have a child around here during the Christmas season," Ann told Ray while they waited for Beth's arrival.

Ray called Champ to walk with him and show Beth around the farm. The large Husky allowed Beth to hug his neck, and he stayed close by her as they walked.

Shorty came from the patio to take a long look at this new visitor, but quickly darted into the garage. Beth ran toward the garage, calling "Kitty cat." Ray tried to coax Shorty out so Beth could see him, but to no avail.

Then Beth saw the horses grazing in the pasture. "Oh, horses! Can I ride the horse?" she begged.

Ray explained to her, "We need to feed the goats right now, but I will let Uncle Bud know that you want to see the horses. That little filly there might even let you sit on her."

All went well until bedtime, and then Beth missed her mom. Ray and Ann distracted her by talking about the goats and reminding her that she would get to pet the horses the next day. Soon she was sound asleep, and the Browns were ready to go to bed too.

Ray awakened early and decided to take care of the animals while Ann cooked breakfast. Champ followed him to the barn. Goldie was in the paddock with the goats; so Ray let Sampson out of the gate to eat near the barn.

Beth soon came to the kitchen all dressed for her adventure on the farm. "Your Uncle Ray is at the barn," Ann told her. "We will eat breakfast when he gets back."

Beth looked out the windows and saw Shorty on the front porch. She quickly went out to pet him.

When the door opened, Shorty took off as fast as a lightning strike. Beth ran after him, but he disappeared before she could see where he had hidden.

Beth saw the barn and remembered the horses. She slipped through one of the cross sections in the pasture gate, and headed toward the horse barn.

Somehow she was able to slide open the large barn door. Once inside, she saw the little filly in the first stall. As she reached to pet him, the latch accidently flipped open.

Out came the filly, glad to be free. She ran through the open barn door into the pasture. "Come back," Beth was calling as she ran after the filly.

When Ann could not find Beth, she stepped out on the deck and called Ray, "Is Beth with you?"

Before he could even answer her, they heard loud screams, "Help! H-E-L-P!"

"That's Beth," yelled Ann as she ran down the steps and headed toward the horse barn.

Champ immediately ran toward the screaming sounds. Before Ray could put down the dogfood and follow, Sampson bounded past him.

Running after the filly, Beth found herself on the backside of the horse pasture. Sensing danger, the filly quickly turned back toward the barn.

As Beth followed, she heard loud growling. There was a wild dog inside the fence, crouched and slowly moving toward her. Beth was terrified!

About that time, Champ lunged and grabbed the beast by the throat. The animal did not know what had hit him because he was focusing on the young girl. Almost immediately, another wild animal jumped on Champ's back.

Moments later, Sampson arrived and knocked that animal off Champ's back. A fierce battle ensued.

Uncle Bud and Aunt Paula had also heard the screams. When all the humans arrived, the dogs' fight was ending. Together, Champ and Sampson were able to stop the wild dogs in their tracks with very little injuries themselves.

Beth was trembling as she ran to Ann, "Bad dogs! They scared me!"

Ann knelt by Beth to give her a hug, thinking, "This child has no idea how close she came to being killed."

After confirming Beth was okay, Ray called the dogs over to check them out. "Good job, Champ! Way to go, Sampson! I'm so proud of you two for saving Beth and the young filly."

Uncle Bud told them that he had been seeing some wild dogs lurking around the edge of the woods, watching his horses. "That's why I started putting them in the barn every night."

The tired dogs followed Ray and Ann back to the house. Ray called the vet and told her about the dogs' encounter. After he answered her questions, she decided, "It doesn't sound like the wild dogs were rabid. How bad are the wounds on your dogs?"

"Considering what just happened, they don't seem too bad," Ray began. "Both of them have some small gashes on their heads and faces."

Dr. Wheeler told Ray, "Go ahead and bring them in so I can check them out...just to be safe."

After putting Sampson back in the paddock, Ray told Ann, "Our brave dogs took care of those wild dogs in no time flat! I am surprised how Sampson was able to hold his own."

The Browns were thankful everything turned out okay. "I'm glad you are safe, Beth," Ann began. "Never leave this house again without letting me know where you are. I don't want you to get hurt."

Ray added, "It is probably best if one of us is with you when you are outside."

Still holding on to Ann's hand, Beth quietly acknowledged she would follow their instructions.

"You can help me feed the goats this afternoon," Ray told Beth. She liked petting Pete.

Beth was able to sit on the filly before her parents came to pick her up.

Ray and Ann shared with Owen and Jean about Beth's narrow escape from the wild dogs. They were also thanking God she was okay.

"When can I come back?" Beth quizzed her parents as they walked out the door.

Beth and the Filly

"I'm sure Aunt Ann and Uncle Ray will need a long break before you come back," Owen responded with a grin. "And, you need to learn more about the dangers of living in the country."

They all waved good-bye as their car drove away. Ray and Ann were both exhausted. Collapsing on the couch, Ray admitted, "Man, I had no idea what a challenge it would be to take care of a small child.

Chapter 18

A STORM IN THE NIGHT

The weather forecast was warning of an ice storm; so, Ray put the goats into the barn. A strong, freezing cold wind blew all night and there was very little movement around the farm.

The Browns awakened the next morning to discover there was no electricity. Ice covered the electric lines, and the wind had blown down some of the heavy-laden wires. Ann would not be going to work that morning. All the schools closed due to the weather conditions.

Ray dressed quickly and went to the barn and paddock to check on the animals. There had been no damage to the barn or the fences, but a tree was down inside one of the paddocks.

Ray laughed when he saw Sampson and Goldie snuggled together under the doghouse roof. "I guess you two kept one another warm last night," he chuckled.

As he returned to the house to report that everything was okay and the animals were unharmed, Ann met him at the door. "Jim just called. Several huge maple trees fell across the pasture fence, and some of his cows have gotten out. He needs you to come help cut up the tree and mend the fence."

"There's so much ice, I'm not sure the roads are passable," Ray warned. "Let me call Luke and see if he wants to go with me."

Luke picked up Ray, and they decided to venture out on the icy roads. Handing the men a box of doughnuts, Ann told them to be careful and give her a call when they got to her brother's house.

The roads were not as icy as they had anticipated, but they did have to stop and remove a pine tree that had fallen across the country road, not far from Jim's farm.

Without much warning, Ray directed "Turn right here! This is Jim's place."

"You are kidding!" yelled Luke. "He lives next door to the farm where my grandparents lived!"

"Really?" exclaimed Ray.

"Yes. That was their farmhouse," exclaimed Luke as he pointed to the house.

They made their way to the broken fence, where Ray introduced Luke and Jim to one another. Ray picked up the chain saw and started cutting away the limbs from one of the trees that had broken the fence.

Luke joined Jim in mending the fence while the new collie rounded up the strayed cows.

"How long have you lived here?" Luke asked Jim.

"About three years," he answered. "I was able to buy the livestock and a herding dog with the farm.

Pointing, Luke quizzed, "Do you know the folks who live on that farm?"

Jim answered, "Ms. Cindy owns that farm now. She just recently moved to town and has put the farm up for sale."

Luke began daydreaming about his adventures in the woods on the backside of his grandparents' property. "My mom's parents lived there when I was a child. The old couple who lived on your farm back then was good friends with my grandparents. I wonder if they are still living."

"We bought this farm from Stacey and Layne Lindsey. If you are interested in finding out if they were the ones who lived here when you were a child, you might want to visit with them at the assisted living facility in town," Jim suggested.

"Are you still having problems with wild hogs?" Ray interrupted Jim.

"Oh, yeah!" began Jim. "A couple of men in the neighborhood have caught some of the wild hogs in traps, but they multiply so quickly it's difficult to keep them at bay."

"I remember how they would tear up my grandparents' garden." Luke admitted, "I was scared to death of those big old hogs!"

"Well, they are dangerous," Jim, added.

Susie brought them some coffee. "Jamie and Mandy can help drag these smaller branches to the woods," Jim suggested. She agreed to send the children out to help.

On their way back to the Brown's farm, Luke asked Ray, "Can you believe that Jim lives on the farm next door to where my grandparents use to live, and he says it's up for sale."

"Are you interested in buying the farm?" questioned Ray.

"That would be a dream come true, but I don't have that kind of money," lamented Luke. "I have some savings built up, but not nearly enough to buy a farm."

Luke's thoughts drifted back to childhood memories of helping his grandfather gather wagonloads of watermelons and cantaloupes to take to the market.

"I was going to talk to you about this later, but I guess it is as good a time as any," Ray began. "I've gotten more calls from people who want timber-frame houses. We are going to be very busy!"

"Alright, that sounds good," Luke responded.

"We're in the process of establishing Brown Construction, specializing in timber-frame building. The architect side of the business is about all I can handle with the goats and dogs too," Ray confessed.

"That Sampson is a great addition to your animal family," Luke interjected into the conversation.

Smiling, Ray continued, "I already have contractor's license, but I would like for you to manage the construction side of our business. It would be a full-time job."

Luke responded quickly, "I really enjoy working with you, and I appreciate all you and Ann have done for me. Tell me more about this new adventure!"

Ray shared, "During the Christmas holidays, Ann and I found an available building located on this side of town that would be a great place for the construction company. My office will remain in my house; so I can keep an eye on the animals. We'll continue running the saw mill and use the storage building, but this new place would house your office and other building equipment."

"I'm interested," declared Luke. "What would be my added duties?"

"In addition to overseeing the running of the saw mill and warehouse, you would be in charge of ordering the supplies and managing the building crews. If all goes as planned, we will need to hire a receptionist/book keeper too," Ray added.

Luke was getting excited about expanding his opportunities, and he felt like he was ready to add on these additional responsibilities.

Ray continued, "If you are serious about pursuing the buying of your grandparents' farm, this job would help you financially, but I'm not sure how much time it'd leave for you to run a farm."

"Oh, that's not a problem," assured Luke. "I'm just thinking about harvesting some of the trees and using the forest to hunt deer and turkeys...and get rid of some of those wild hogs."

They arrived back at the farmhouse. They agreed to talk more about the business after the purchase of the construction building was final.

As Ray got out of the jeep, he shared "There's something else you might want to consider. My dad is a banker, and he helped Jim with a loan for his cow farm. Let me know if you'd like to talk to him about a loan."

Luke was so excited he sang all the way back to the trailer. He told Logan all about the new job offer and the possibility of moving to a farm...his grandparents' farm!

The sun came out after lunch, and some of the ice was melting and dripping off the roof of their house. Ray checked Pete and Patsy to make sure they were dry and ready for another night in the barn.

"Maybe tomorrow it will be dry enough for you to get out into the paddock," Ray encouraged the goats.

Sampson and Goldie were checking out the fallen tree when Ray came to feed them. He decided to leave the tree on the ground in the paddock. Pete and Patsy would enjoy eating the leaves and climbing on the tree trunk.

As they prepared for the dark night, Ann started lighting candles all over the house. Just as she lit the last candle, the electricity flickered back on.

They were grateful to be able to watch the news on television before going to bed.

"Thank God for electricity," whispered Ann as she slid under the warm blankets.

Chapter 19

VISIT INTO THE PAST

Luke was interested in seeing inside his grandparents' farmhouse. He called Milly to set up an appointment. She had several meetings scheduled in the city, but she was able to get one of her agents to meet him at the farm that afternoon.

He really liked the renovations, and he was very interested in buying the place, but he still had to work out the financial details.

Ray took him to the bank where his dad worked. "Dad, this is Luke Patrick."

Extending his hand, Ray's dad said, "Hi Luke. I'm Guy Brown. Jim's told me all about this farm you are interested in buying."

After discussing the financial options, Mr. Brown encouraged Luke, "I think with the down payment you have saved and the full-time job you now have at Brown Construction, you should be able to get a loan to cover the remaining cost of the farm."

Rising quickly from his chair, Luke grabbed the banker's hand, "Thank you! Thank you! I appreciate your help so much!"

Mr. Brown chuckled, "Well, don't celebrate yet. We still need to follow through on your loan application." As they were leaving, Mr. Brown thanked Luke again for his service in the military.

All the paperwork was finally in place for Luke to purchase his grandparents' old farm. A closing date was set and he could hardly wait to make it officially his own farm.

In the meantime, Luke decided to follow through with Jim's suggestion to talk with Mr. and Mrs. Lindsey. Jim called and informed them that the young man who is buying Ms. Cindy's house would like to come by and talk to them about the farm. They agreed on a time, and Luke was on his way.

Mrs. Lindsey greeted Luke at the door and led him into the kitchen where Mr. Lindsey was sitting in a wheelchair.

"Excuse me for not getting up, young man. Jim tells me you are buying Cindy's farm."

"Yes Sir," Luke began. "My grandparents lived there many years ago, and I was wondering if you knew them."

The doorbell interrupted their conversation. It was Cindy. "I'm sorry. I didn't know you had company."

"Come on in. This young man is here to talk about your farm."

"Oh, I'm sorry, it's already been sold, and we will be signing the paperwork in a few weeks," Cindy informed them.

"Yes. I know. I'm the one who is buying the farm," informed Luke. They all had a good laugh as Cindy and Luke quickly introduced themselves to one another.

"Before the doorbell rang, you were asking me if we knew your grandparents," Mr. Lindsey stated. "Who are they?"

"Annie and Allen Gregory," Luke shared.

"My soul, boy, they were our best friends," exclaimed Mrs. Lindsey. "We were saddened when they sold their farm and moved to Louisiana."

"Dave and I bought your grandparents' farm when they moved," Cindy chimed in. "Which one of their daughters is your mom?"

"Mira," Luke answered.

"My sister, Leigh, and I grew up playing with your mom and her sister, Jan," Cindy explained. "In fact, Mira and I were best friends. We communicated with one another until your family moved to Germany. We lost touch after that."

Luke could hardly take it all in. The Lindsey family knew both his grandparents and his parents too!

"Tell us about your family," encouraged Mrs. Lindsey. Luke told them that his grandparents were no longer living. He shared all about his parents' move to Colorado and his recent visit with them, his sister Marie, and Aunt Jan.

As Luke drove back to his farm that afternoon, he kept thinking about his informative visit.

"I am buying my grandparents' farm from their own best friends' daughter. Who could have ever guessed that such a thing would happen?" He was amazed!

Chapter 20

NEW ARRIVALS

Over the past few weeks, the Browns had noticed Patsy's utter rounding out, and she had become less active. Anticipating her kids would be born soon, Ray got Patsy situated in the "birthing" area of the barn so she could get familiar with the new surroundings.

Ray checked on Patsy every morning, and Ann visited her in the afternoon. In addition to the fresh hay and water, she ate a special grain.

In their research, the Browns read that it was important to be present when possible and monitor the birthing of baby goats, in case anything went wrong. They both planned to be there to help.

Before going to bed, Ray went to check on Patsy one last time. She seemed more unsettled than ever. She had pawed the bedding into a nest and was circling around nervously. He came back to the house to tell Ann that he was going to stay in the barn for a while.

"Okay. I think I am going to try to sleep some. I have a busy schedule tomorrow. Call me if anything happens," instructed Ann as she gave Ray the birthing kit and towels they had prepared for this big event.

At the stroke of midnight, Ann received a call from Ray, "Ann, come quickly, Patsy's having a kid!"

When Ann got to the barn, she could hear Patsy bleating. The water bag had burst, and they soon saw the nose and two front feet coming out. In a few more minutes and after several more strong contractions, a healthy male kid was born. They watched Patsy lick her newborn son dry and nudge him with her nose.

Ann suggested, "Let's name him Midnight!" Glancing at his watch, Ray agreed.

Ray tied off the umbilical cord about an inch from the belly with strong sterile thread. He then cut the cord just past the thread and covered the umbilical stump with Betadine.

"Dr. Wheeler says it will need to be treated twice a day for the first two days," he told Ann.

Midnight struggled to his wobbly feet. Ann guided him toward Patsy's teats so he could get a small milk snack. He then snuggled down in the soft hay by his mom.

Ray offered Patsy some warm molasses water. "The water will rehydrate her, and the sugar gives her energy, he told Ann.

Patsy had not rested very long before the contractions and heavy panting started again. "I think Patsy is having another baby!" Ray told Ann.

They were a little more prepared for the birthing of this second male kid. He presented himself differently, but he expelled quite quickly. Soon, he made his way to his mom's teat and began nursing.

"It's Valentine Day; so let's name him Valentine," Ray suggested as he offered some special grain to Patsy.

The nanny was still restless. She would lie down, get up, walk around, lie down and repeat this several times. "What's going on with Patsy?" Ann quizzed.

"She's acting like she's trying to deliver another kid," suggested Ray.

About that time, a tiny goat head appeared. This time the kid did not deliver as quickly as the first two, and Ray had to help Patsy. Membrane covered the newborn's head. The small kid was sputtering and trying to cough up mucus.

"Something's wrong!" Ray shouted as he anxiously picked up the kid by the hind legs, letting the mucus drain from the throat and mouth. He encouraged the little goat, "Come on now, breathe...take a breath. There you go!"

Wrapping the tiny goat in a towel, Ann announced, "It's a girl!"

"What are we going to call her?" questioned Ray.

"How about we name her Angel?" Ann suggested.

"I think that's an appropriate name for this special little gift from heaven," agreed Ray.

Ann gently placed Patsy's third-born baby by her mom. Patsy was exhausted and did not want to have anything to do with this baby.

Ray talked quietly to Patsy as he gave her some water with electrolytes that helps nannies hydrate during times of stress.

Once Patsy had settled down, Ann tried to get the baby girl to nurse. It took some coaxing with squirts of goat milk on her mouth, but Angel eventually started nursing.

Ann joined Ray on the stall floor. "That was scary!" she whispered.

"Yes, it was!" Ray agreed. "Three baby kids! Patsy, your first litter is triplets!"

Even though the early morning adventure had been exciting, the Browns were tired and sleepy.

Once the baby goats were all asleep, Ann went back to her own bed. Ray brought a camping cot into the barn and set it up near Patsy. "Let's get some rest," Ray whispered as he fell asleep.

Chapter 21

VALENTINE DAY

February 14 was also the closing date for the farm Luke was purchasing. He stopped by the Brown's barn to observe their newborn triplets on his way to Carroll Real Estate.

Luke was excited that he would soon be the proud owner of his grandparents' farm. The receptionist took him to the conference room when he arrived.

Milly came in to share some news. "Mr. Brown tells me that your loan request has been approved, but the total of your loan has been changed."

Luke was concerned, "What do you mean?"

"Well, apparently the seller knew your grandparents when they owned the farm. She told me that she just could not charge you the same price as she would a complete stranger. So, she's lowered the price on the farm!"

"Wow!" Luke was grateful.

"Cindy and her daughter are on their way," Milly informed Luke. "It shouldn't take too long for us to get your signatures on all these papers. Then you can move into that special farm."

Luke looked up from the paperwork placed in front of him when two women walked in. He was surprised.

"Lynn! What are you doing here?" They had not seen one another since he returned from his Christmas vacation.

"Lynn is my daughter," informed Cindy.

"Thank you for lowering the price on the farm," Luke began. "I really appreciate your kind gesture."

It took a while to sign all the papers, and Luke was having trouble keeping his mind on the paperwork.

His thoughts were swirling, "If Lynn is Cindy's daughter, then that means Mr. and Mrs. Lindsey are her grandparents. Could she be the girl I played with during the summers on my grandparents' farm?"

Milly gave Luke the farmhouse key she had and told Cindy, "Now you can give Luke all the other house keys that you have."

"Oh, no," Cindy exclaimed as she looked frantically though her purse. "I must have left the extra keys at the house."

Lynn quickly suggested, "I can bring them to you on my way out to the Brown's farm to see those baby goats."

"Okay, I'm going straight to my farm now," informed Luke. "I'll see you there."

Luke was moving his things into the farmhouse when Lynn drove into the driveway. "Hey, I appreciate your bringing out the extra keys."

Smiling, Lynn responded, "Oh, I was headed out this way anyway, and besides I want to show you something."

Following Lynn around the farmhouse and toward the forest, Luke ventured a question, "Where are you taking me?"

"Just wait and you'll see," Lynn responded. Luke soon saw the creek.

Pointing to the large oak tree by the edge of the creek, Lynn shared, "When our moms were children, Grandpa tied a rope on that limb. All of the children and grandchildren enjoyed that 'Tarzan swing' for years. We'd swing across this creek on the rope and fall into the cool creek water," Lynn continued.

"I remember doing that too!" Luke interrupted.

Lynn led him to the tree, "This is what I wanted to show you." There on the old tree trunk was a heart-shaped carving with two letters carved in the middle of the heart.

"You are my childhood playmate!" Luke declared. Looking at the big smile on Lynn's face, Luke questioned, "How long have you known?"

"I remembered your name was Luke, but I didn't know your last name. My suspicions were confirmed when you recently visited my grandparents."

Luke admitted, "My hope was if I could find the elderly couple who lived next door to my grandparents, then I could find their granddaughter. When your mom said that she and my mom were best friends, I suspected her daughter had to be the one I played with while visiting the farm. Then, when you walked into the real estate office today, I was pretty sure it was you!"

Sharing their childhood memories and laughing together felt so comfortable for Luke and Lynn. He gently took her by the shoulders, "Hey, it's Valentine's Day and we need to celebrate renewing our friendship, and my big purchase. Will you go out to eat with me tonight?"

"I'd love to do that, but it will have to be a late dinner. I am chaperoning a dance at the middle school where I teach. You could go with me to the dance, and then we can eat afterwards." Lynn suggested.

Luke happily agreed, and she headed over to the Brown's farm to see their Valentine surprise...three baby goats!

Lynn could not wait to tell Ann all about her own Valentine surprise!

Chapter 22

KID GOATS

Business was going well at Brown Construction, and Ray was happy with Luke's leadership in the company. They both missed the times when they could just sit out on the porch and visit for hours. In addition to the full-time job and keeping up his own farm, Luke was spending more time with Lynn.

The Browns were busy themselves. Taking care of the three new kids took more time than anticipated. They were checking on the goats often.

"The goats want to nurse all the time," Ray observed. "But, it seems Angel has given up on nursing."

Angel stood with her head hanging down while her brothers took over their mom's teats. It was evident that the bigger, stronger, and pushier ones took advantage over the smaller one.

Clearly, Angel was not able to get her fair share of milk. The Browns had to intervene. It was a struggle, but they fed her a few tablespoons of colostrum every two hours that first day. In a couple of days, the young kid was drinking almost a pint two times a day.

Dr. Wheeler brought a disbudding iron to show Ray how to burn the goat buds into inactivity. She told them that her goal for the kids was that they double their weight in two weeks.

Ann was glad she was at school when the disbudding happened. She did not think she could watch them doing this to the small animals.

Dr. Wheeler was quick to inform them that disbudding was a way to protect the goats and the people who take care of them.

Goats naturally use their horns and head to butt, and they tend to get their horns hung in the fences or thick brush. Neither of these were good.

Patsy produced a lot of milk; so, Ray would be able to take some for drinking once the kids were over two weeks old. Mr. Jordan agreed to teach them what to do.

He told Ray to separate Patsy from the kids overnight, and he came out the following morning. They positioned Patsy in the special milking stall, and began practicing.

Ray collected a small pail of milk, and Ann took it inside to refrigerate. Then, the kids were able to nurse on demand all day long.

"Goat milk is creamy and smooth because the fat globules are smaller than cow's milk. It is naturally homogenized," Ray informed Ann.

She finally ventured a taste, but was not fond of it as was Ray. He liked drinking a cup of cold goat milk before going to bed each night.

At first, the kids ate fresh good-quality hay and a mixed grain with molasses twice a day. Soon they were able to go outside so they could get more exercise and munch on brush and grass. Pete seemed glad to have their company.

Ray watched Sampson's behavior when he brought the kids into the paddock. The young Pyrenees was curious and sniffed the kids, but followed Goldie's lead.

Eventually, Ray separated the male and female goats. They all wore blue lightweight snap on collars to signify they were from the same family.

Valentine and Midnight were in the same paddock with Pete and Sampson. Angel was in another paddock with Patsy and Goldie. She liked being with her mom, but she missed playing with her brothers.

Milly wanted to see the baby goats, and it had been months since Snowball had visited the farm. She called to set up a time the Browns would be home.

Champ met them, barking loudly as he greeted Snowball. Their barking awakened Sampson from a short nap just as Snowball exited the vehicle.

Wide-eyed and staring, Sampson thought, "WOW! He quickly ran to the fence and started barking too.

Milly led Snowball to the fence and introduced her to Sampson. The two Pyrenees touched noses through the fence, and he was smitten.

To Sampson's great disappointment, Milly then led Snowball toward the house so she could play with Champ on the front porch. Sampson sat with his eyes glued on the vehicle, hoping not to miss seeing Snowball when she came back.

In the days ahead, he thought about Snowball often and hoped she would soon visit the farm again.

Sampson and Snowball

Chapter 23

ESCAPE

Ann and Ray arrived home from church one Sunday and were surprised to see Pete in the driveway. The farm watchdog had positioned himself between Pete and the road, barking loudly. Uncle Bud's grandsons were running toward Pete.

Ray quickly jumped out of the car and yelled for the boys to stop running. He thanked Champ and tried to calm Pete, gently coaxing him to stand still.

Once he was able to grab the goat's collar, Ray walked him back to the pasture. There he found Goldie and Sampson keeping Patsy and her three kids corralled in the paddock.

"What happened?" Ray quizzed the two young boys.
"We came to see the baby goats," Wayne explained. "And somehow the big goat got out."

Ty added, "I closed the gate when we left; so, I don't know how he got out."

Ray explained, "Just closing the gate will not keep the goats inside the fence. Goats can use their noses to unlatch the gate if it is not locked."

Red-faced from trying to catch the goat, the boys apologized. "You didn't know about the lock," Ray responded. "I'm just glad none of the other animals got out."

The young boys were invited back to visit the kids anytime, but Ray repeated to them again that they had to be careful to lock the gate when they leave.

To ensure there would be no more escapes, Ray went around checking all the gates. He wanted to make sure they were locked securely.

"Those boys could have been hurt," declared Ann.

"Yes. I'm glad nothing worse happened," responded Ray.

He petted Goldie and Sampson as he was leaving the paddock, "Good job keeping the other goats safe."

It was still dark outside when Ann got ready for school the following morning. The light from atop the large goat barn allowed her to see the goat pasture.

There looked like an animal lying near the outside of the fence. At first, she thought it must be Champ.

She then noticed another small animal struggling to stand up. Looking more closely, she realized it was a deer doe with a new fawn.

Ann could not wait to tell Ray!

He joined her in the kitchen as she was leaving. Sleepily, Ray explained, "The doe probably felt safer near the dogs. I heard coyotes barking all night; so I suppose she was running from them."

As Ann slowly drove out their driveway, she could not see the doe and fawn anywhere. She was disappointed Ray had not gotten to see their animal visitors that morning even though he'd seen other deer in the woods before.

Chapter 24

EXTRA, EXTRA

All their research made the Browns more interested in animals. Some people even called Ray the "animal whisperer". His kind-hearted manner seemed to calm dogs, goats and other animals in his care. It was common for people to call him or come by for advice.

Uncle Bud was looking for a burro to put in the pasture with his horses, and he asked Ray to go with him to the local stock barn. As they entered, an older man approached them saying, "Aren't you Ray Brown?"

Surprised, Ray nodded his head, wondering what this man wanted with him. "I hear you know a lot about goats," the man continued.

Chuckling, Ray said, "Well, my wife and I have done a great deal of research. What do you need?"

"I have this solid black goat that is wild," the man shared. "I don't know what to do with her!" He gave Ray his address and asked if he would come by and observe this crazy goat of his.

Once at the old man's farm, Ray could see that he had tethered the wild goat to an iron pole staked inside a paddock with no other goats. Ray stood at the fence watching this doe repeatedly choking herself as she would run away from the pole as fast as she could...only to get jerked back when she reached the end of the rope.

When her owner placed water and food within reach, she turned it over and kicked the containers.

"You have a challenge here for sure," Ray said.

"I would be grateful if you would just take her off my hands," begged the bewildered man.

After a short phone call to Ann, Ray agreed. "I do have an extra paddock where I can put her, and I'll be glad to see what I can do."

Ray accompanied the old man into the paddock and started talking to the goat as he moved slowly toward her. When he reached for the pole to untie the goat, she lowered her head and ran toward him.

Quickly moving out of her way, Ray put his foot on the rope, shortening the goat's travel space. She was startled when "the choke" came sooner than she anticipated.

The men finally got the wild goat tied inside the bed of Ray's truck. They were exhausted, and the goat seemed tuckered out as well.

Ann met Ray at the paddock, opening the gate so he could get the goat situated in her new living space. At first, Ray thought he might put her in the paddock with Angel and Patsy, but he was afraid she might hurt them.

He told Ann, "This wild goat could probably take care of herself even without a dog in the pen with her."

Before releasing the new arrival into the empty paddock, Ray exchanged the heavy leather collar that was around her neck with a red light-weight snap on one. She ran freely in the paddock and seemed to be okay with being alone.

In the days ahead, Ray left hay and grain for the wild goat, but she would only eat the grass growing in the paddock. Fresh water was available whenever she would make the effort to drink. She stayed as far away from him as she could get.

"It's like she was never around people or ever fed any food," Ray told Ann. "I'm going to see how she responds to being in the paddock with the female goats."

He helped Goldie herd Patsy and Angel into the same paddock with the wild one.

For weeks, the black goat would not go near the other goats nor come near Ray when he visited. Often, he walked through the paddock pulling down limbs so the goats could eat the leaves.

Sometimes, Ray would break off a small branch and throw it toward the black goat, trying to encourage her to eat the leaves. He continued talking calmly to the strange goat, trying to get close enough to touch her.

Even though she had not had anything to do with him nor the other goats, Ray saw her butting heads with Angel one day.

"It is evident she knows about the goat pecking order," he told Ann.

To everyone's surprise, the black goat joined Patsy and Angel at the manger one morning.

Later, she came with the other goats to greet him when he opened the gate into the paddock. He could see her relaxing a little more every day.

Ray finally decided to take a chance, reached over Angel, and touched the wild goat on the back. It was a non-threatening way for him to pet her, and she did not run away.

Ray moved Patsy and Angel back into their original paddock so he could try to feed the wild goat some sweet grain. As he walked slowly back through the gate and into the paddock, Ray talked to her calmly.

"Come try some of this sweet food," he coaxed, shaking the pail of special grain. He sat down on a stump and held out the pail, waiting for her to come eat.

Ray's patience paid off. She walked slowly up to him and smelled the grain. Sticking her head into the pail, she started eating.

"It's good, isn't it," Ray whispered. This became a daily ritual for a week.

After that, Ray moved the black goat to the paddock with the other female goats. What a celebration the Browns had when they were able to water and feed the rehabilitated doe with the other animals.

Ann suggested, "Let's name her Sascha."

"Where did you get a name like that?" laughed Ray.

"When I was young, we had a solid black cat named Sascha," began Ann. "That cat looked and acted like a wild animal. I couldn't begin to tell you all about Sascha's crazy antics."

"I'm okay with naming the goat Sascha, but let's hope her wild antics are now over!" Ray responded.

As they were walking back to the house, a family friend called Ann to share the sad news that her son and daughter-in-law were in the midst of a divorce.

"They need to find a place for their three goats," she explained. "They have two nanny goats and a male yearling. Would you and Ray be able to take these goats?"

After discussing the possibility of adding three more goats to their growing herd, Ray and Ann agreed to drive to an adjoining county and get the goats.

They took two different colored lightweight collars to keep the goat families separated from one another. They put yellow collars on one nanny and her yearling. The other nanny received a white collar.

"More goats?" thought Champ as he followed Ray's truck to the barn barking.

When the two nannies entered into the paddock with the female goats, Sascha walked away to the far side of the paddock. She was still cautious of new things, but nothing like when they first brought her to the farm.

Pete greeted the yearling as he came into the male goats' paddock. Midnight and Valentine were playing on the rocks. They paid no attention to the new arrival.

Sampson and Goldie soon checked out the new additions to the farm. The goats did not seem frightened of the dogs at all.

"We now have nine goats!" Ann exclaimed as she shut the gate.

Before they left the paddock, Ann's phone rang. It was the previous owner of their three new goats.

"I need to tell you that both of the nanny goats have recently been bred," he shared.

Wide-eyed and in shock, Ann turned to tell Ray the surprising news. Speechless at first, they both started laughing. The possibility of having even more goats around the farm in a few months was a bit overwhelming for both of them.

Chapter 25

UNEXPECTED

Ann and Lynn met in the crowded teachers' lounge for a cup of coffee before beginning classes.

Lynn leaned over and whispered, "Do you remember the opera singer I told you about?"

"The one who left you in New York?"

"Yes. He called me last night," Lynn shared.

"From Paris?" Ann was surprised.

Lynn motioned for Ann to follow her out of the room. "He's back in New York for an opera, and he wants me to come audition for it as well."

Quickly glancing around the hall to make sure they were alone, Ann questioned, "Are you going?"

"I don't know," began Lynn. "I've missed singing in the Metropolitan, and this could be a great opportunity to get back into the opera scene."

"What about Luke?" Ann could not help but ask.

"He's actually the only reason that I am struggling with a decision to leave. Mom is settled in town now, and the final music class concert is this Friday night."

"How much time do you have to make your decision?" Ann asked.

"I probably need to make arrangements within the next week," informed Lynn.

"I want you to be happy, but I will really miss you if you decide to leave," shared Ann. "And, I don't think you will find a better man than Luke."

Tears were welling up in Lynn's eyes as she slowly walked away.

Unaware of Lynn's struggle with making such a difficult decision, Luke was planning a way to get rid of the wild hogs on his property.

Ward brought his rusty old trap to Luke's farm and helped him scope out a good place to set up the small enclosure.

They scattered corn inside for the hogs to eat. Their hope was that when they came inside to eat, the trap door would close and capture some of the swine nuisances.

"Now you will have to check it every day," directed his old friend.

Luke promised he would look at the trap every morning before going to work. He would add corn if needed.

Early the following morning, Luke called to Logan, "Let's go see if we caught any wild pigs." He grabbed his rifle and they jumped into his truck.

As they neared the area where they had set up the trap, Ray could hear a loud commotion of squeals and grunts. It was soon evident they had caught something...a full-grown boar hog!

The huge black menace was lunging at the steel bars with tremendous force. Logan jumped from the truck and headed to the trap. His growling and barking agitated the captured hog even more.

Luke was not sure how much longer the temporary prison cell would contain this fierce animal. Just as he took his rifle from the truck, the angry boar burst from the broken gate of the cage and headed straight toward him.

Logan tried to cut off the hog and fought with all his might, trying to keep the huge animal from Luke.

The wild hog was a relentless attacker, slicing the dog with the two sharp tusks protruding from his mouth.

Luke fired a shot at the charging boar, but the bolt jammed and the rifle went flying into the air on impact. Luke hit the ground in excruciating pain.

Logan jumped on the hog's back, biting his ears until the relentless aggressor slung him to one side. This distracted the hog long enough for Luke to get his service revolver out of its holster.

Wild Boar

Luke emptied all nine bullets into the hog's head at close range, finally stopping the dangerous beast.

Logan drug his badly wounded body closer to Luke and collapsed. They were both bleeding profusely from the wounds inflicted by the wild boar.

Luke quickly tore off his t-shirt and wrapped it around his leg. He was unable to walk and knew he had to have help. He managed to get his cell phone from his pocket and call Ray.

Feeling faint, Luke put his arm across Logan's lifeless body, thanking his faithful friend for saving his life yet again.

Luke heard a noise and saw Ward's jalopy appearing in the clearing nearby. His old friend saw the three bodies lying on the ground, and could see the seriousness of Luke's condition.

Before Ward could get out of his truck, Ray arrived, leading an ambulance into the war zone.

The EMTs immediately attended to Luke and quickly rolled him to the ambulance.

"Don't worry about your dog, Buddy. I'll take care of everything," promised Ward as the door to the ambulance shut.

A doctor met the ambulance upon its arrival and began working on the new patient. Luke could not remember much about his first hours in the emergency room. All he could think about was his great loss.

He could not imagine life without Logan. Both he and his dog healed from previous wounds during the war and continued their mission. This time, his faithful canine friend did not survive the attack.

He awakened to a familiar voice, "Luke, can you hear me?"

Struggling to open his eyes, Luke saw a nurse he knew. "Janet, what are you doing here?"

"How are you feeling?" she quizzed.

"Like a 10-ton tank just ran over me," he responded.

"Well, you lost a great deal of blood," informed the nurse. "Your wounds have been cleaned and sutured. We are giving you a broad-spectrum antibiotic."

Hospital personnel allowed Ray to go in and visit with Luke. When Janet came in to check on her patient, he introduced her to Ray.

"This is Janet Barton. She and I met in Germany," Luke started. "She took care of me when I was injured in the war."

Janet smiled, "We were more than nurse and patient."

Luke explained to Ray, "She and I dated for about a year after I got out of the hospital."

Then, Luke questioned the nurse, "I don't see a ring. Are you not married yet?"

"No," she responded. "How about you?"

"Not yet, but I've been seeing a woman for about six months now," he informed her. "We actually knew one another when we were children."

"I heard you had gotten out of the Marines. I'd like to spend some time catching up later," she suggested as she walked out of the room.

Ann and Lynn bumped into Janet as they came running into the room.

Simultaneously, the women asked Luke, "Are you okay?"

Lynn was in tears as Luke explained what happened. He had incurred lesions on his thigh and arm.

"There is a slight possibility of getting rabies from a wild hog injury," Ray informed. "To make sure the boar was not rabid, the caucus was taken to the College of Veterinary and Animal Science for a postmortem."

"When will they know the results?" Ann asked.

"I'm not sure," responded Ray. "I think all they have to do is check the hog's brain for the rabies virus."

Janet returned to tell Luke's guests that they have to leave soon because he needs to rest.

Luke looked away as to gather his composure. "Logan did his best to protect me from that wild hog."

All three friends shared their heartfelt condolences for Logan's passing, and Lynn hugged Luke good-bye.

The two teachers had ridden to the VA hospital together, and Lynn was glad to have some time to talk on their way back to the school.

Lynn planned to discuss with Luke that night about her new invitation to New York. Because of the accident, that conversation was not going to happen.

"What if he has rabies?" Lynn burst out in tears. "I can't lose him!"

"While we wait for the results, let's just hope for the best," Ann encouraged.

"I can't leave Luke like this," Lynn continued. "I care too much for him to take off to New York right now."

After dropping off Lynn, Ann drove home thinking about her friends. "I hope Luke recovers well and Lynn doesn't regret passing up the opportunity to sing again in the Metropolitan," she mumbled to herself.

At dinner, Ann told Ray about Lynn's invitation and her struggle to make a decision. "I think Luke's medical situation has shown her how much she really cares for him."

"You know that nurse taking care of Luke?" Ray shared. "She and Luke dated about a year."

"What?" Ann was shocked.

Ray continued, "Yep. They seemed happy to see one another again. I think they may try to get together when he gets out of the hospital."

"Oh, no!" exclaimed Ann. "Lynn is giving up on her dream to sing opera in New York again because of her feelings for Luke, and he's getting reacquainted with an old girlfriend!"

As difficult as it was, the Browns agreed to stay out of Luke and Lynn's love life and see what happens.

They were all overjoyed to hear the good news that there was no rabies detected in the boar's brain.

When Luke's stay in the hospital was over, Ray drove him home. On their way to the farm, Ray ventured a question about his relationship with Janet.

Luke assured Ray, "I'm in love with Lynn, and I don't want to do anything that will hurt our relationship."

Ray could not wait to tell Ann about Luke's confession. "Thank God I did not say anything to Lynn about that nurse," sighed Ann.

It took a while for Luke's physical wounds to heal, but he was back at work sooner than they expected. He was lonely on the farm without Logan.

Talking with his old friend about times with his faithful dog helped some. Luke appreciated Ward taking care of

Logan's body. They planned a memorial service for the war hero.

A granite headstone was made for the dog's grave. Lynn and the Browns joined the two veterans at the special service. A flag was hanging half-mast on a pole located nearby the grave.

Lynn shared with Ann how thankful she was that she decided to stay. Later, she told her, "I saw on Facebook that my opera friend is engaged to someone he met in Paris."

Smiling, Ann responded, "I told you that you could not find a better man than Luke."

Lynn agreed.

Chapter 26

ADDING SNOWBALL

While drawing house plans at his desk, Ray heard the phone ringing in the kitchen. It was Milly. "Ray, I need you to come help me with Snowball."

"Okay. What's going on?" he quizzed.

"I tripped and fell down the steps as Snowball and I were leaving for our morning walk," she explained between gasps of pain. "My neighbor has called 911."

"I'm on my way!" assured Ray. "Have you called Ann?"

"She's in class right now. I left a message on her phone," Milly sounded frantic.

On his way to the truck, Ray called the school and asked them to give the message to Ann. He arrived at Milly's house just as the EMT's were immobilizing Milly's arms and right leg.

Ray assured her that he would take care of Snowball. He quickly put the young dog in her crate so he could follow the ambulance to the hospital.

Ann soon joined them in the emergency room. They waited together as doctors came to check Milly's injuries. She was in great pain.

After x-rays and exams, it was determined that one wrist was broken and the other one had a moderate tear to the ligament. Medical personnel soon attended to both injuries.

Milly's hip was also broken. The doctor scheduled surgery for early the following morning and admitted her into the hospital.

Ann planned to spend the night at the hospital with her mom, but she needed to go back to the school and get things ready for her next day's substitute.

Milly requested Snowball stay at her house until they find out more about her recovery. On his way to the farm, Ray stopped to feed the lonely Pyrenees and spend some time with her.

It was getting late and Ray needed to take care of his own animals. He gave Snowball a hug before putting her into the crate.

Ann called the next morning to tell Ray that her mom's surgery went well. She was coming home long enough to get a shower and change clothes.

Ann told Ray that the doctors advised Milly to go to a rehab facility straight from the hospital.

"We'll need to keep Snowball at our place," Ann informed Ray.

"Can she stay in a paddock or do I need to bring her crate to the farm?" asked Ray.

After some consulting with Milly, Ann told Ray to go ahead and try Snowball in a paddock. They could decide later as to whether they would need to break down the crate and move it to the farm.

Ray thought putting Snowball in the paddock should be easy since she has already met all the farm animals.

Champ greeted Ray and Snowball at the truck when they arrived. All of the dogs seemed happy to see Snowball, and Sampson was frolicking around as if he was excited she was there.

Ray kept Snowball on a leash while he walked her around the empty paddock. He talked with her about Milly's situation and told her that she will be staying awhile on the farm.

He then removed the leash and stayed in the paddock for a while. Snowball stayed close to the fence nearest the other animals, barking constantly. Goldie kept an eye on her as she made her rounds inside the paddock with the female goats.

Snowball quickly moved closer to the fence when Sampson came to greet her from the paddock where he was taking care of the male goats.

"Hum...you two Great Pyrenees should become good friends," Ray smiled to himself.

Leaving a rawhide bone for the young dog to chew on, Ray went back to the house. He later brought a "kiddie pool" into her paddock and filled it with water. Snowball stood in the cool water lapping up some of the water.

"It would probably be more fun if you had a buddy playing with you," Ray observed.

Periodically, Champ came to visit Snowball through the fence from outside the paddock. Having her friend nearby helped Snowball feel more relaxed, but she whined when he left her.

Ann came home from the hospital late that afternoon. "How's Snowball doing?" she asked.

"I think she likes having the other dogs nearby," Ray shared. "I don't know if she's nervous or bored, but she's barking a lot."

"Maybe we can put her in the barn tonight and see if that helps," suggested Ann. Snowball managed to settle down enough to spend the night in the paddock.

The following morning, Ray decided to take her on a leash walk in the paddock where Goldie was guarding the female goats. His biggest concern was how she would react to the goats.

Ray reprimanded Snowball when she would bark at the goats and pull at the leash. By the time he took her back to the empty paddock, she was able to observe the goats in the other paddocks without jumping up on the fence.

Each day, Ray took Snowball for a leash walk into one of the paddocks where there were goats. She did quite well adjusting to her surroundings, but she did miss Milly.

Weeks passed and Milly's recovery was slow; she was getting frustrated. Ann took Snowball to the rehab center a couple of times, but she was always pulling at the leash, wanting to return to the farm.

Observing the young dog's behavior, Milly told Ann, "You don't have to bring Snowball back. I'll see her when I get out of the rehab center."

As he did with Sampson, Ray started taking Snowball into the paddocks without a leash. He observed her while he gave fresh water to the goats. Except for wanting to hang around Sampson when they went into his paddock, she was doing well obeying Ray's commands.

"I think I'm going to put Snowball in the paddock with Goldie," Ray announced one morning. "If she does as well as Sampson has, she should turn out to be a good goat dog."

Chapter 27

A PLAYGROUND MENAGERIE

The Browns recognized that goats are super smart and get bored easily. Their ancestors were mountain climbers; so they love to climb anything they can. There were already rocks and stumps in the four paddocks, but Ray wanted to build some awesome structures to keep the goats entertained.

First, Ray hung a swinging platform from the limb of a large shade tree in the paddock nearest the barn. Not only did the goats play and relax on this structure, but the dogs also lay under it during hot weather.

Luke helped Ray roll four old truck tires into one paddock, and they secured them in the ground in a stand-up pattern. The agile goats seemed to like jumping through and balancing on top of the tires.

Ray also built a three-sided hut with a flat roof. In addition to having a dry place to go when it rained, the goats could lounge on the top. The active goats could access the wooden shelter by a ladder or a slide.

Ann laughed at the goats pushing one another off the goat teeter-totter that Ray built in another paddock. She saw several goats racing up the step platform made from logs. It seemed they enjoyed eating the bark from the logs as much as resting there.

Goat playground apparatuses

Oberhasli goats are associated with the Swiss Alps, and Ann suggested Ray build a playhouse menagerie that was in keeping with the Swiss theme. He drew up plans for a magnificent goat chalet he wanted to build in the paddock nearest to the road and farmhouse.

Luke came over early one morning to help construct the goat chalet. It had bridges and platforms, steps and slides and a tall tower with window openings on the sides of the goat house.

"I need to bring Lynn out here to see all of this," declared Luke.

It was hilarious watching the goats going in and out, up and down. There was no mistaking their joy of playing on all the new climbing apparatuses inside the paddocks.

Ray opened the gates to different paddocks each day, giving the goats opportunity to spend time on all the playthings.

Often, vehicles would stop on the side of the road so their occupants could watch the goats playing on and in their playground menagerie. The Browns noticed an old grey truck parked on the side of the road by the goats' Swiss chalet several times a week.

Goat Playground Menagerie

Ray was cleaning out the chalet one afternoon when the old grey truck pulled up to the fence and stopped. Two children jumped out and came to the fence to observe the goats closer.

A young man slowly emerged from the truck. "Hello. I'm Adrian Gonzales." Pointing back at the vehicle, "This is my wife, Bella, and these are our sons, Jorge and Philippe."

"Good to meet you," Ray responded.

"Our boys like your goat farm," Adrian began. "We live on the old Cooke farm."

"Do you have goats on your farm?" quizzed Ray.

"Not yet, but I'm planning on raising Boer goats one day. They are good meat goats."

Ray shared, "It'll take a while for the Boer goats to get big enough to sell, but I hear that there is a great demand for goat meat. So, it can be a profitable small farm venture."

Getting the Gonzales' sons back in the old truck took some time because they wanted to stay and pet the goats. Ray brought Pete to the fence and let them pet him before their parents insisted they had to go home.

Ray told Ann about his visit with the Gonzales family. "I want my students to come see the animals too," she told Ray.

Soon after the new school year began, Ann scheduled a Saturday afternoon for her students and their families to come to their goat farm. They were able to pet Pete and give snacks to all the goats. Even their parents enjoyed observing the goats on their playground while Ray lectured on "caring for goats".

Finally, the last family left, and the Browns locked the gates. "I think your students had fun," Ray told Ann.

"Yes. The goats aren't the only ones who enjoy their playground menagerie," Ann responded. "I think any one of the children who came today would be happy to have a playground just like this." Hugging Ray, she said, "Thanks for helping me make today special for my students and their families."

Chapter 28

DANGER LURKING

The Gonzales family had been busy getting their farm ready to bring home some goats. Even the children were helping to put up a fence and clean out the old shed in their backyard. They had begged their parents for months; they wanted some goats as pets.

Although he would not be popular with his boys, Mr. Gonzales' plan was to have Boer goats to breed and sell. They would raise them for meat and later breed them so they could have milk to drink while the Boer goats get big enough to sell.

Finally, the fence and shed were ready for the goats. The children were excited when their dad brought two Boer goats home from the stock barn.

Mr. Gonzalez tied the young goats to the fence post so his sons could pet them. Once untied, the goats ran around checking out their new surroundings.

It was getting late, and it was bedtime for the children. They did not want to leave the goats outside. Their mom and dad promised they could play with the goats after breakfast the following morning.

These unsuspecting parents were unaware that there was a wildcat family hiding deep in the forest near the Gonzales farm.

The four wildcat cubs had been nursing, but now they were getting big enough for meat. It had been a challenge for their mama to run deer or hunt small animals as she usually did because one of her back legs had been badly injured in a trap.

That night, while searching for a meal for her family, the female cat happened upon the Gonzales farm. She had maneuvered herself into the backyard when one of the goats appeared from the shed.

Suddenly, the chickens started clucking and screeching, flying around inside the barn, causing a ruckus. Adrian peered out the window to check on the goats.

There was a full moon; so, he was able to see that one of the goats was out of the shed, walking around in the paddock.

Grabbing his gun, he stepped out on the porch just in time to see a huge black cat pounce on the goat and take a couple of leaps toward the fence.

A quick aim and the gun fired! There was a loud scream from the cat, but she held on to the goat as she barely cleared the fence.

Limping, the wounded mama cat drug the young goat slowly back to the den where her cubs tore into the fresh kill. They devoured the goat and there was nothing left for their mom. She desperately needed rest and food for herself.

Licking her wounds, the weary cat knew that she must move her cubs. Putting some distance between them and the scene of the kill was driving her to keep going.

Bella joined her husband outside as he was checking on the other goat. "It was huge! I'm sure it was a cat, solid black," explained Mr. Gonzales. "The thief took one of our goats! I must have hit the cat because I heard a loud scream as the gun fired."

The wild animal had taken the female goat, and the upset dad found the male one safely tucked away in the corner of the shed. They locked him inside the shed for the night.

Neither of them was able to get any sleep. They knew that their boys would be upset to learn of the missing goat kid. They briefly discussed what they could do to keep this remaining goat safe.

Adrian was determined to try to follow the cat tracks when it was light outside, but his wife begged him not to go into the woods alone.

A knock on the door startled Ray. He was not expecting anyone, and he had not heard the old truck driving into the driveway.

Visibly shaken, Mr. Gonzales began telling Ray all about the sad event that happened on his farm the night before. "I think it was a panther!" he exclaimed.

"Are you sure it was a panther?" Ray quizzed. "They usually live deep in the woods and are rarely ever seen. Only a few farmers in this area claim to have seen what they identified as a panther. In fact, some think it's just a mythical animal like Big Foot."

"What I saw was real!" exclaimed Mr. Gonzales. "It was a huge solid black cat, and it carried off our young female goat!"

"I'm so sorry you lost one of your goats. Is your dog okay?"

Hanging his head, Mr. Gonzales shamefully responded. "I don't have a dog. After buying the two Boer goats, I didn't have enough money to buy a dog."

"The mere presence of a dog would have deterred the wild cat. I'm glad you still have your male goat," declared Ray.

Reluctantly, Mr. Gonzales asked, "Could you keep the one goat that I have on your farm until I can get a dog?" Ray helped him put his young goat in the paddock with his own male goats and handed him a business card.

"Here is the address of a rescue shelter nearby. You can probably adopt a good herding dog there. That's where we got Sampson."

"I can work on your farm as payment for you keeping my goat," Adrian offered. "Do you like eggs? We have chickens, and I can bring you eggs too."

Ray called other farmers in their community to tell them what had happened at the Gonzales farm. He advised them to be aware the large black cat was injured.

An injured wildcat is more likely to be looking for easy targets. Goats hemmed up inside a fence are easy targets unless there are dogs inside the paddock with them; so Ray felt his goats were safe.

Just as a precaution, Ray moved all of their goats to the front two paddocks nearest the house, and he kept a gun by the back door.

Since Valentine and Midnight were usually playing together, the yearling was happy to have the Boer goat to accompany him around the paddock. Pete usually lounged on one of the platforms, watching the young goats playing.

Mr. Gonzales was able to find a dog at the rescue center, and the Boer goat only stayed two weeks at the Brown farm.

It was a happy day for the Gonzales family when their goat returned home, and they now have a dog to protect him.

The yearling at the Brown farm was lonely without his Boer goat friend. He moped around, and never joined the others on the playground. Ray tried to console him, petting his head and talking to him every time he visited the goats.

It had been three weeks since the Gonzales' female goat had been taken from their farm. No one had reported any other sightings of a black cat; so Ray was relaxing a little, hoping the wild cat had moved far away from the community.

One of the nannies was restless and looking like she was close to delivering her kids; so, Ray put her into the birthing area of the barn. He wanted to get her acclimated to the area before the big event of delivering her kids happened.

Leaving the nanny inside, Ray flipped on the large spotlights located on the outside of the barn. These bright lights made it possible to see inside the paddocks, even in the dark.

As was customary each night before going to bed, Ray stood looking out one of the large bedroom windows, watching the dogs periodically running around the perimeter of each paddock where they were assigned. Snowball was in the paddock with Goldie and the female goats, and Sampson was guarding the male goats.

All three dogs were taking their responsibility seriously and were doing a great job of checking out the paddock and keeping the goats safe.

He did not see Champ making rounds outside the large perimeter pasture as he had done so many nights before.

Recently, Champ had been guarding the Brown's farm from their front porch.

It looked like most of the goats were already asleep, lying inside one of the goat huts or under an overhang. All was quiet and calm.

Ray had no idea that at that very minute a 200-pound wild cat was hiding in the branches of an overgrown tree limb that reached out over the outside perimeter fence of the paddock where the male goats were now resting. She had been carefully watching Sampson's ritualistic run around the paddock, awaiting a chance to pounce down on a goat.

Before getting her paw caught in a trap, the wild cat could have leapt 20 feet, easily clearing this barbed wire fence, even with a goat in her strong jaws. Mr. Gonzales' shot hit the injured leg and now, she barely has the use of only one back leg.
The wild cat was planning a quick kill and return back up the leaning tree limb, making her exit the same way she arrived.

Seeing the yearling wandering around alone, she determined he would be her easiest prey. Creeping further down the limb, the anxious cat poised herself for a pounce onto the goat.

The yearling turned and went back toward the lean-to where the other goats were sleeping. Hurting and hungry, the huge female cat was getting impatient. She strategically decided to take a chance on running down the goat if he came any closer.

The wild cat fixed her eyes on the yearling and waited for an opportunity to attack. Unaware of the danger that was lurking in the tree, the yearling started walking toward the cat.

Goldie saw the black cat sailing through the air from the tree limb, and began barking and running toward that direction. Immediately, Sampson headed toward the cat as she was gaining ground on the run-away yearling.

Ray heard all the dogs barking ferociously. He grabbed his gun and headed outside. He could hardly believe his eyes as the commotion before him played out like a horror movie.

The huge black cat seized the yearling, breaking his back. Grabbing the goat with her mouth, she turned to head back toward the tree limb. Much to her surprise, Sampson was there, blocking her way. He was crouched, barking and lunging toward her.

The determined cat started toward the nearest fence, hoping she could get across with the goat in her mouth. By that time, Champ had left the comfort of the porch and arrived on that side of the paddock. He jumped up on the outside fence, growling and barking at the wild cat.

Desperate, the hemmed-in cat turned away from the fence and tried once again to make it back to the safety of the tree.

Ready to fight, the dangerous cat dropped the yearling and turned to face Sampson. She started swiping at the approaching dog with her large front paws. He managed to spring back in time to miss the damage those long sharp claws could have made.

Ray tried several times to shoot the dangerous animal, but could not take a chance of hitting Sampson.

Then as if in slow motion, Snowball leapt onto the roof of the goat shed in her paddock, propelling herself over the inside fence into the pasture where the action was happening.

Snowball surprised the wild cat with a rear attack, sinking her canine teeth into the cat's hip. Feeling the excruciating pain running up her leg, the angry wild cat, tried to spin around and get loose.

The large cat was now lying on her back, trying to bite the relentless dog and fighting with her razor-sharp claws. Snowball was holding on with all her might.

Sampson took the opportunity to grab the wildcat's throat with his trap-tight jaws. His goal was to obliterate this murdering intruder. The sounds of screaming, growling and barking were horrendous.

Soon, the fight was over. Releasing the lifeless body, the two Great Pyrenees stepped back to view their enemy.

Ann had been watching the frightening event through the large bedroom window. Sobbing, she soon joined Ray in the paddock. He was checking Sampson and Snowball's injuries. Both dogs were covered with blood.

Most of the blood on the dogs turned out to be the cat's blood. In Snowball's zeal to help Sampson, she had incurred some cuts on her face from the cat's claws.

Ann helped Ray clean up the dogs and treat Snowball's wounds. It was late; so they decided they would call the veterinarian in the morning.

Ray and Ann were both saddened by the loss of the yearling, but thankful that their dogs and remaining goats had survived. He wrapped up the young goat and placed it in the barn so it could be disposed of properly the following morning.

Shining a flashlight on the massive 6-foot long black cat, they noticed that she was a "mama cat".

"She was trying to get food for her cubs," Ann declared.

"She must have been desperate for food if she jumped into this paddock knowing there was a dog here," Ray told Ann.

Pointing, Ann whispered, "Look at our tired, brave dogs." Sampson and Snowball were resting under the lean-to, watching the goats sleeping.

"They sure make a great team," Ray responded. "Now that everything has calmed down, I'm going to leave Snowball in this paddock for the night."

The following morning, Dr. Wheeler came to the Brown farm to check on the two Pyrenees heroes.

Ray called Luke to tell him about the wild cat and ask if he could come over to help search for her wild cubs. Getting a good sniff of the huge cat, Champ tore off into the woods. In no time, the men could hear him barking.

They found four cubs bedded down in the thick brush, awaiting their mom's return. Ray decided not to disturb them.

He called the Department of Natural Resources to tell them about the wild cubs. Several hours later, a large truck from Fish and Games Services arrived.

Ray led the two men to the place in the woods where they had discovered the hungry cubs. They put these cubs into crates and rolled them to the large truck.

Ray asked the men if these cats were Panthers.

"No," the driver replied. "These four cubs are black Cougars."

"What will happen to them?" Ray quizzed.

"Researchers at the University will want to examine them, but they will probably be raised in a zoo," the man replied.

Ray was anxious to inform the neighbors that the injured wild cat was no longer a threat. He first called Mr. Gonzales and told him that the wild cat was a black cougar.

All of the farmers were relieved to know that the lurking danger had been taken care of...for now anyway.

Chapter 29

SURPRISE, SURPRISE, SURPRISE

Snowball's injuries had healed, and she continued spending her days divided between helping Goldie with the female goats and guarding the male goats with Sampson.

Ann's mom returned to her house from the rehab center, and she could not wait to visit the farm and see Snowball.

"I'm so impressed," Milly announced. "Snowball has become a goat herding dog while I was recuperating."

"Yes, she has," agreed Ann.

"Actually, she's a very attentive goat dog," Ray added. "I don't know what would have happened if she hadn't helped Sampson take down that large cougar!"

"Mom, we'd like to keep her on the farm," Ann declared.

Observing the dogs and goats for a few minutes, Milly finally responded, "I think Snowball would be bored silly at my house now, but I will miss her terribly."

Ann encouraged, "Well, you can come visit her here anytime you want."

Both of the pregnant nanny goats gave birth to two kids each. The first one delivered a male and a female kid. Three weeks later, the other nanny gave birth to twin male kids. There were now 12 goats on the Brown's farm.

In addition to their regular jobs, Ray and Ann were busier than ever taking care of the new kids and all the other animals on their farm. They hardly ever spent time with Luke and Lynn.

Early one morning, Luke called to invite Ray to eat lunch in town with him that day. He wanted to talk about a project he needed Ray to help him with.

First, Luke had Ray swear not to tell anyone, not even Ann, about his special plan. Then, he excitedly shared with Ray that he is planning to ask Lynn to marry him!

The old oak tree that was located on the property line between Luke and Jim's farms was a special place for Luke and Lynn. He wanted to "pop the question" to Lynn there at the tree, but he wanted to first convert the area into an enchanted place.

Luke had already gotten permission from Jim to make changes in the area, and now he needed Ray to help draw up his ideas on paper. As he talked about it, Ray drew up the plans.

Looking at Ray's drawings, Luke exclaimed, "Yes! That is exactly what I imagined! I'll take the trees from my property, but I will need to use the old saw mill if it's okay with you."

"Sure. Do you have a date in mind?" Ray started. "I mean, how long do you have before all of this has to be finished?"

"My goal is to have everything completed before Lynn's birthday; so I have less than a month to get it all done," answered Luke.

With everything at the Brown Construction Company so busy, there was very little extra time to work on his special project. Eventually, Jim came over to help, and Luke was finally ready to invite Lynn to his home for her birthday dinner surprise.

Lynn arrived at Luke's farm as the sun was going down. He led her down a lantern-lined pathway toward the old oak tree. He instructed her to keep her eyes on the pathway until he told her to look up. As they reached the top of the incline, Luke said, "Now, you can look."

Lynn could hardly believe her eyes! The tree was completely lit up with tiny lights woven in and out of every limb. There was a picnic table sitting on a circular "porch" that went around the base of the tree. There were yellow balloons tied to flower pots located around the entire structure.

As they got closer, Lynn saw a picnic basket and a covered cake plate sitting on the picnic table. A lit lantern was in the middle of the table highlighting her birthday dinner and a vase of red roses. She was speechless, trying to take it all in.

Then she saw a swing. "You put up a new swing!" she yelled. The swing had a large padded seat with ropes covered in blue satin ribbons.

"And it's big enough for both of us to swing in it together," Luke shared.

Like two young kids, Luke and Lynn ran toward the swing and sat down by one another. Pushing back as far as he could, Luke pulled up his feet and they soared out over the creek. The reflection of lights on the water was magical.

"It's wonderful," whispered Lynn as they swung out over the creek repeatedly.

"Are you hungry?" Luke asked. Lynn nodded her head. They dismounted the swing, and walked toward the picnic table.

Luke stopped by the tree where they had carved their initials so many years ago. He quickly knelt with ring in hand, declaring his love for Lynn, asking her to marry him and make his childhood dream become a reality.

In tears, Lynn knelt beside him, "Yes! I'll marry you. It was my childhood dream as well," she confessed.

What a special night, eating her birthday dinner under the tree by the creek, remembering their times together playing there as children and thinking about their lives together as adults, soon to be husband and wife.

The wedding date was set for less than a year away, and everyone was happy for Lynn and Luke. He asked Ray to be his best man, and Lynn asked Ann to be her maid of honor.

Lynn's mom was anticipating a grand reunion with her childhood friends when Luke's mom and aunt returned for the big wedding.

As time drew closer to the wedding, Ann was busy planning and hosting wedding showers for them. She was exhausted and started going to bed earlier and earlier each night. Ray was concerned, but she assured him that she was just tired.

He came in one afternoon and told Ann that he thought Snowball was going to have puppies. "Dr. Wheeler is coming to check on the baby goats tomorrow; so, I will get her to check Snowball too."

Smiling, Ray continued, "We've had quite a few baby goats born here on the farm, but this will be our first litter of puppies to be born here."

Once the news got out that Snowball was going to have puppies, several family members and friends put in their requests for one of the puppies.

Ann began experiencing flu-like symptoms. Many students had been out of school sick; so she thought she might have caught something there. She took time off from school so she could get some rest. They hoped she would feel better each day, but she was still not feeling well.

Ray convinced Ann to call and make an appointment with the doctor, just to be sure. The doctor's schedule was full; so, it was several more weeks before she was able to get an appointment with him.

"I'm putting Snowball in the infirmary section of the barn tonight," Ray shared with Ann one afternoon.

"Is she sick?" quizzed Ann.

"No. She's dragging, and I'm thinking those pups are going to be born any day now," Ray shared.

The day finally came for Ann to see the doctor. She was being examined when Ray texted her. As soon as she was out of the doctor's office, she read his message. "Snowball has just delivered six pure-white healthy puppies!" Ann could not wait to get home and see them.

Running to the barn, Ann joined Ray by Snowball's side. The barn door to the paddock was open so the other dogs could come see the new additions to the Brown farm.

Sampson stood proudly by Snowball who was nursing the puppies. Goldie quietly gazed on the six puppies as if she were their loving grandmother.

Holding the runt of the litter in his arms, Ray said, "Aren't they the cutest puppies you have ever seen?"

"Yes. They are as cute as they can be!"

"They are so fluffy. I just love cuddling them!" Ray shared.

Ann responded, "It's a good thing you're getting experience cuddling the baby pups because you will be cuddling your own baby in a few months."

Ray stopped rocking the puppy and looked at Ann. "What did you just say?"

Laughing, Ann repeated, "In a few months, you'll have your own baby to rock and cuddle!"

Ray quickly placed the puppy by Snowball and grabbed Ann's hands. "We're going to have a baby? Are you okay?"

"Yes, I don't have the flu. My body's just preparing for our baby to grow," Ann answered. "The baby and I are just fine."

Ray picked up Ann and swung her around. "We're going to have a baby! We're going to have a baby!"

With arms around one another and tears running down their cheeks, Ray and Ann paused to thank God for His special blessings. They were especially grateful for the news that they will soon be having a long-awaited healthy baby of their own.

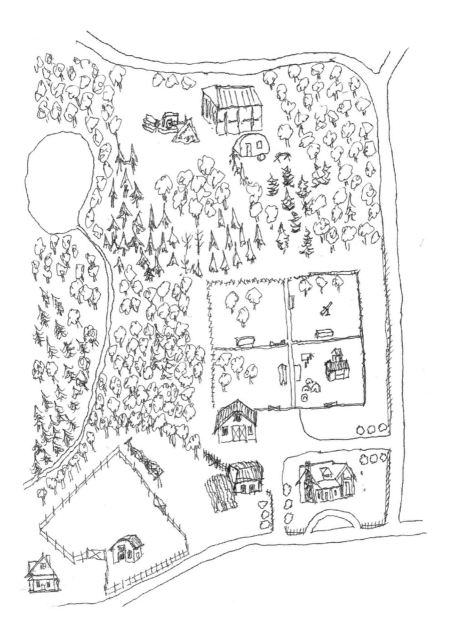

The Brown Farm

ABOUT THE AUTHORS

Glenn and Camilla Dyer grew up in Georgia. They met in college where they obtained degrees as professional educators. In addition to raising two children of their own, they worked with thousands of young people.

Camilla was a teacher and school counselor. Glenn was a teacher, coach and youth minister. They also served as Youth and Singles Consultants in Europe.

Although they are retired, the Dyers teach and mentor adults, and participate in community service organizations and their local church.

Glenn, a cartoonist, does woodwork, loves to sing and often teaches art classes at an art gallery. He has illustrated three other books.

Camilla enjoys needlework and writing. Both authors have written articles for a recreational magazine.

The Dyers are also excited about their next book, Six Pyrenees Puppies. Be watching for its publication.

Made in the USA
Columbia, SC
27 June 2021